A Love Shared

A LOVE SHARED

CHRISSIE LOVEDAY

THORNDIKE
CHIVERS

This Large Print edition is published by Thorndike Press, Waterville, Maine, USA and by AudioGO Ltd, Bath, England.
Thorndike Press, a part of Gale, Cengage Learning.
© Chrissie Loveday, 2010.
The moral right of the author has been asserted.

LIBRARY OF CONGRESS CATALOGING-IN-PUBLICATION DATA

Loveday, Chrissie.
    A love shared / by Chrissie Loveday. — Large print ed.
        p. cm. — (Thorndike Press large print clean reads)
    ISBN-13: 978-1-4104-3716-7
    ISBN-10: 1-4104-3716-7
    1. Large type books. I. Title.
PR6112.O79L68 2011
823'.92—dc22   2011005110

BRITISH LIBRARY CATALOGUING-IN-PUBLICATION DATA AVAILABLE

Published in 2011 in the U.S. by arrangement with Chrissie de Rivaz.
Published in 2011 in the U.K. by arrangement with the author.

U.K. Hardcover: 978 1 445 83672 0 (Chivers Large Print)
U.K. Softcover: 978 1 445 83673 7 (Camden Large Print)

Printed in the United States of America
1 2 3 4 5 6 7 15 14 13 12 11

A LOVE SHARED

A Stranger's Kindness

Sarah struggled to push the bale of hay towards the feeding manger. It was hopeless. Once more she cursed her painful, broken arm. Major, her beloved stallion whinnied and nuzzled her good shoulder.

"You can just stop that," she ordered fondly. "If it wasn't for the accident, I should be out with you right now." He snuffled against her once more and she let the bale drop to the ground as she patted him. "Beautiful boy, aren't you." She loved everything about her horse. His smell. His warmth. His magnificent looks.

Horses were so comfortable in their own skin. It fitted perfectly over the smooth muscles and shone in the autumn sunshine. "All the same," she murmured. "I have to do something about this ridiculous situation." She half dragged, half pushed the bale of hay towards the manger, not even daring to think of how she could get it off the ground once she reached it.

Major gave a whinny. Sarah looked round as she saw that someone was riding past the gate of her small paddock. It was a strange horse, a rather magnificent grey. She knew most of the people around here who had horses but she recognised neither horse nor rider. He, the rider, looked as imposing as the horse. He was wearing a well cut tweed jacket and beautifully tailored jodhpurs. The obligatory helmet covered his head and shaded a large part of his face.

"Are you having problems?" he asked rather fatuously. He leapt down from his horse in an easy, graceful movement and flipped the reins over the horse's head, hooking them onto the gate post. "Here, let me get that for you." He hefted the bale of hay into the manger as if it weighed nothing and smiled down at her. "Looks like you need more than a bit of casual help. How did it happen?" he asked, nodding towards her injured arm.

"Some mad maniac on a motorbike came charging down the bridle path and scared the life out of both of us. Major panicked at the sudden noise and I went down like the proverbial ton of bricks." Subconsciously, she brushed aside her unruly mop of hair in some vain attempt to make herself look less of a tramp in front of this perfectly turned-out rider.

"Did you catch the biker?"

"No chance. He was off and gone. Fortunately, Major didn't wander and I was able to lead him back, this useless arm hanging down. I managed to get him back into the field and then I sort of passed out. Someone driving by saw me and luckily, stopped and came into the field. Poor Major was standing over me like a protective angel."

"Good heavens. Sounds dreadful."

"It was at the time. Joe called the ambulance and managed to unsaddle Major. Joe's one of the local farmers, so he's used to livestock. Major's very gentle anyway. Just large."

"He's a beautiful specimen. So, you were carted off to the hospital and the arm set?"

"Yes. They kept me in overnight, as I live alone. That was six days ago."

"I assume you live somewhere nearby?"

"I have a cottage just back there and I rent the paddock."

"Look, why don't you let me take care of Major, until you're on your feet again? Or should I say back with a functioning arm. There's plenty of room and feeding two horses isn't any more effort than seeing to one."

"Oh I couldn't possibly," she mumbled, blushing. How could she let a stranger, however dashing, look after her beloved horse? "That's very kind of you, but I can manage." He stared at her with cool grey eyes, looking her up and down. She was clearly fibbing. She could no more manage to look after a large horse than do a hand-stand at this present time.

"Suit yourself then. See you around, no doubt." He strode back to his own mount and leapt easily into the saddle. He gave a cursory wave and trotted off.

"Thanks for the help," she called after him, but he was out range. She looked down at her scruffy, grubby jeans and the old but-toned jacket pulled over her plastered arm and realised what a spectacle she presented. "So," she murmured to Major, "who do you think he was? Rather an amazing sight and a gorgeous mare with him. I bet you liked the look of her too."

She gave a small sigh, half regretting the fact she had turned down his generous of-fer, but sensing her instincts had been right to refuse. She really had no idea who he was, nor how he could manage to be out riding on a weekday morning. Landed gentry, was a cliché that sprung to mind. She'd certainly remember if she'd seen either him or his mare before.

The horse was clearly a thoroughbred and he spoke with a rather cut-glass accent that suggested private education and money in the background. All the same, her own dear Major was worth far more than money to her and she couldn't bear him stabled somewhere she didn't know.

All the same, he must have thought her very odd. A scruffy female with dirty hair and covered in bits of hay. Somehow, she needed to sort herself out. Do something about her hair for a start and organise some clothes she could manage to get on and off with one arm. Being right handed and with a broken right arm, life was indeed difficult. Usually, she was smart, always well turned out and with her enviably slim figure, usually set a high standard for the entire office.

She walked home. She shivered in the cold autumn air. It wasn't far but she wasn't used to walking even this short distance and there was no way she could drive. She had tried working at home using her left hand to type on her computer but it was difficult, inefficient and an absolute pain.

Her clients would have to make do with phone calls for the rest of this week. It would be at least another six weeks before she could drive again, so after a few more

11

days of enforced sick leave, she needed to find a way to get into work at the solicitor's office in the nearby town.

She specialised in family law and had many people who relied on her. Also after a few more days and she might feel more able to see her clients again, if of course, she could first sort out her own appearance. It wouldn't do for a respectable solicitor to be seen in scruffy jeans and an old button-through cardigan, in the office.

The answering machine was flashing when she got back home. Her mother. No doubt fussing again for her to go back to stay with them. She played the message and dialled her number with an air of resignation.

"Hi, Mum. Returning your call."

"Darling, how are you?" Her tone conveyed sympathy and exasperation all in one go. Her mother specialised in such tones.

"I'm fine. Managing just fine."

"And is the pain a little less?"

"Getting there. A few things are difficult and of course, I can't drive yet."

"Then why on earth don't you . . ."

"I know, come back home and let you wait on me. I can't, Mum. I shall be going back to work soon. Once I can organise a lift, at least I can dictate letters and see my clients."

"I bet you're not feeding yourself properly

and that horse of yours will be taking up all your time. How on earth are you managing him?"

"I'm getting the odd bit of help," she replied, blessing the man who had stopped just a few minutes ago. It saved her from really fibbing. "Actually, someone has offered to stable him for a few days."

"Thank heavens. We've been so worried you'd do yourself even more damage trying to manage him. When does he go?"

"He isn't. I mean, I don't know this person at all. He just happened by when I was putting hay out."

"But it sounds like a perfect solution."

"Maybe if I knew the man . . ."

"Oh, a man was it?"

"Oh Mum, stop that. No, I mean yes, he was a man, but I've never seen him before and I would never let Major go anywhere I didn't know or let just anyone look after him."

"I don't know where you get your stubbornness from. You get an offer which gives you the perfect solution and you turn it down. Find out who the man is for goodness sake. Check him out. He might just be the answer to your prayers."

"Or yours," she muttered. Her mother was constantly nagging her to find herself a nice

13

man with whom she could settle down. And doubtless produce babies for her to coo over. As if her sister's three weren't enough. "How's Beth and the tribe?"

"She's fine. They're coming for lunch on Sunday. Why don't you join us?"

"Can't drive, remember?"

"We could organise something. I'm sure there's someone who could give you a lift. Your new friend for example."

"I don't even know his name. But I'll see you soon, Mum. Must go. Love to Dad and to Beth and Mike and the kids. Bye."

Sarah put the phone down before her mother could launch into a new tirade. She loved her parents, but she was in no mood to face another badgering to return home. She could manage. Of course she could manage. At twenty-nine, she was quite old enough to manage without her parents' help.

OK, so Beth had produced her three boys by the time she was this age, but Beth was not career-minded. She and Mike had been childhood sweethearts and had never wanted anything more than to be married and have a family. Nothing at all wrong with that. She just wished her mother could accept that she preferred a career and that she had done well to reach the position she had, at her age.

Specialising in family law, she felt she had made a large contribution to the firm's work and had always tried to deal fairly with the local community who came to her for advice. She put the kettle on and spooned coffee into her favourite mug.

As she sat by the fire, electric as it provided instant heat, she dialled the number of her hairdresser.

"Lesley? Hi, it's Sarah. Sarah Pennyweather. I wonder if you could fit me in for a cut and blow-dry. Soon as possible, please. I've broken my arm so I can't do much and it's looking a dreadful mess."

"I can do tomorrow morning if that's any good. Nine-thirty."

"Great. I'll have to get a taxi and then call one to return me when I'm done."

"No problem. We can organise the collection taxi for you when you're finished. See you at nine-thirty tomorrow. Thanks. Bye."

Sarah hung up and settled back to enjoy her coffee. She looked for her notepad and a pen. Then realised she couldn't write left-handed. She always had lists. She lived by lists. Jobs to do on a daily basis.

Since her accident nearly a week ago, she had been doddering through the days. Her main concern was looking after Major, but

15

her usual routine had gone to pot. The normal day began at six-thirty when she went to the paddock and made sure he had food and water. When it was cold at night, she shut him in the stable but that hadn't been necessary, so far. It was still warm so she could leave him outside.

By seven-fifteen, she had usually showered and was eating her breakfast of fruit and muesli, washed down with coffee. Then it was drive to the office and be ready at her desk by eight-thirty. Organised. Efficient. For the past week, she had been getting up around nine, flung on her oldest clothes and made coffee and breakfast. She'd wandered down to the paddock and then spent the rest of the day reading or even watching daytime television.

She realised she was in danger of getting hooked on the various property programmes and then found herself looking forward to whatever rubbish people were digging out of their attics to sell to provide some treat or other. It was a dangerous situation, she told herself.

She was removing herself from everything she believed in and becoming hopelessly distanced from her normal days. All the same, she might just watch the programme where they were doing up a whole house in

16

a ridiculously short time. Just as she was settling down, the phone rang. She recognised the office number.

"Hi Sarah. It's Poppy. How are you getting on?"

"Oh, you know. So, so. Thanks for asking. Still can't drive and getting bored and frustrated by how little I seem able to do. How are things at the office?"

"Erm, well . . . Actually, I'm ringing to say that we need you to come in. Tomorrow morning. There's a full practice meeting. Nine o'clock sharp."

"But I can't. I can't drive. And anyway, I have an appointment."

"Sorry love. It's urgent. No excuses. You'll have to take a taxi."

"What's going on?"

"Sorry. Can't say. Just get here tomorrow. Bye."

Sarah listened to the dialling tones after Poppy had rung off. How strange. Usually, the receptionist-cum-secretary was so friendly and chatty. She was the public face of the partnership. This demand was decidedly off. Damnation. She would have to cancel the hair appointment and, oh dear, much worse, go into the office looking an absolute mess. She dialled the hairdresser again to get an earlier appointment.

That was one problem solved. The next was to find something she could wear, that would look halfway decent over a cumbersome plaster. What on earth was so urgent that she needed to go to the office when she was on sick leave? She'd been away for less than a week. What could have happened in that short a time?

Poppy had been very mysterious. She wondered whether to phone one of the others but decided against it. Maybe she'd really prefer not to know what was going on until tomorrow. No, she would tackle her wardrobe problem, and she must remember to book a taxi. She was hopeless without her lists telling her what she needed to do. The usual smart suits she wore for work were useless.

The best she could manage was a plain camisole top and a loose jacket hanging over one shoulder, teamed with a pair of smartish trousers. It would have to do. It was only a meeting tomorrow, after all. She could always buy something else in the town, after the meeting.

She pondered over the reason for the urgent meeting. She'd heard nothing on the office grapevine about any changes. It must be something and nothing. She grilled some cheese on toast and remembered her mother's words about feeding herself properly. She would wander into the village this afternoon and stock up at the village shop. They must have some fresh vegetables and fruit. Need to eat my five a day, she reminded herself.

Sarah rose at six the next morning. Her hair was looking so much better. She'd gone for a much shorter than usual look and it gave her confidence to face the ordeal ahead. Lesley had done a great job.

A sluice under the shower and a quick brush through would suffice. Much easier than the usual shoulder length bob that needed so much care to keep it looking sleek and in good condition. Mind you, the plastic bag she used to cover her plaster was making even showering tricky.

She had spent time with Major the previous afternoon and had decided to stable him as it looked like being a cold night. All she needed to do this morning was to let him out and feed him his favourite treat of apples. The little tree in her garden was loaded with fruit this year, so it was all very easy. Supplies were on hand. She walked down to the paddock and saw Major was sheltering in his open stable.

The beautiful stallion whinnied his pleasure at seeing her and she gave him the apples. She watched as he charged across the grass, enjoying the open air. She smiled and went back to the house. She changed out of her scruffy clothes, quickly made some instant coffee and munched her muesli. It was already past eight o'clock and her taxi would be arriving soon. How much longer everything took one handed.

Everyone in the front office welcomed her arrival. There were sympathetic comments along with questions about her work load and queries as to when would she be back.

"What's all this about?" she demanded.

"Changes afoot, we understand. Nobody seems to know much," Poppy told her. "Love the hair, by the way. Suits you."

"Thanks. So, where are we meeting?" Sarah asked.

"Boardroom, of course. I've been told to organise coffee in there. You can go in and have a cup if you like. I'm not sure if anyone else is in there. Place seems to have been deathly quiet since I got here. We're starting at nine. Everyone's to meet in there to begin with. Phones in answering mode. Then the office staff move out and the rest of you continue till whenever."

"All sounds very mysterious. Nobody's died have they?"

"Not that I know. Anyway, you go and grab yourself a coffee and somewhere decent to sit. We'll be in soon, once we've received the grand summons."

"OK. Thanks." She pushed the door open with her good hand and went through the narrow corridor to the boardroom. It was exactly what one would expect from an old fashioned solicitor's company. Oak panels. Vast table, polished within an inch of its life and large leather seats that were so heavy she could barely move them.

She poured a coffee from the heated jug and stood by the window. She would sit to one side, near the opposite end of the table to where the senior partner would be. The door opened and Charles Talbot came in. He was a younger member of the team, about the same level as she was but generally thought of as a bit of a pain.

He was also what the secretaries described as something of an octopus. He always put his arm on a shoulder or rested his hand somewhere unwelcome. He thought of himself as an irresistible ladies' man. His aftershave was intense and cloying and Sarah tried to edge away from him.

"Sarah, my darling. You've been sorely missed. No sunny smiles around the place and your in-tray reaching skyscraper proportions. We should get together one evening very soon. We need to discuss the implications of this shambles today."

"What do you know? What's going on?"

"New man in the team, I gather. All I know. Senior management just got bigger."

"But who . . ." She got no further as the door opened and the rest of the staff trooped in. She nodded at the familiar faces and stared at the one unfamiliar face. Everyone helped themselves to coffee and she went to sit down near to Poppy and the other girls, partly to avoid being too near Charles and his aftershave. The side door opened and the senior staff came in. The meeting was ready to start.

A New Work Colleague

Ken Milligan, the senior partner in the firm of Milligan, Jones and Partners, led the party into the boardroom. There was a stranger among the group, a youngish, tall, extremely good-looking man, with dark hair and silvery grey eyes. His broad chin had a look of strength and he had a generous, ready smile.

Though now impeccably dressed in a dark suit and elegant silk tie, he looked slightly familiar to Sarah. But she was not the only female staring at him with interest. He certainly made a most attractive addition to the dark suited group of men.

"Good morning, everyone," Ken said in his beautifully modulated voice. He was always immaculate and had distinguished silvery grey hair that always impressed in the court rooms of the county. "Firstly, let me thank you all for being present so promptly and a special thank you to Sarah for interrupting her sick leave to be here."

Sarah blushed slightly and nodded her acknowledgement. The new man looked at her and she saw a flicker of recognition slip across his face. This was her rescuer of yesterday, she realised. They nodded at each other as they both reached the same conclusion. What ever must he think of her? She had been somewhat brusque when she turned down his kind offer to look after Major.

"May I introduce Alex Weston? He is to join us as one of our senior partners from today. As you must all realise, I am rapidly aging and looking forward to retiring. Some of you may also know that my dear wife is unwell and is to undergo surgery very soon. So, partly because of this and also because of my own wish to ease the workload, I am going to work part time only, from now on.

Very much part time."

There was a murmur around the table. Ken was a popular boss and would be sorely missed. Sarah wondered how the other seniors would feel about this newcomer's arrival in the higher ranks. It was clear that he would most probably be taking over as head of the firm, in due course. Still, if he was a keen rider, in Sarah's estimation, he couldn't be all bad.

Ken coughed for attention and continued.

"I'll leave Alex to introduce himself and tell you a bit about his background. He is extremely accomplished and has an excellent track record. Alex Weston, ladies and gentlemen."

There was a small ripple of nervous applause, as Alex rose to his feet. Even without the added height of a riding helmet, Sarah could see that he was tall.

Around six feet at least, she estimated. His height was possibly exaggerated by his slender build. She had the vision of him leaping from his saddle the previous morning, clearly athletic and obviously very fit. She almost missed his opening words and came to as he was speaking of his move to this Cornish town as the fulfilment of a long held ambition.

"Inevitably, there will have to be some

24

changes in the structure of the firm to take account of the current difficulties in the financial world, but with a bit of reorganisation, everyone's jobs should be safe." He continued to speak of his experience in other solicitors' firms. There were a number of reactions to his words and Sarah noticed some discomfort amongst the older members of the group.

This newcomer was clearly a high flyer and very ambitious. "Finally," he continued, "let me say how much I look forward to getting to know you all and working with you." There was another ripple of applause and Poppy leaned over and muttered,

"He can get to know me any time he likes."

"You're dreadful, Poppy," Sarah hissed. "What about that gorgeous fiancé of yours?"

"I was only thinking of my usually boring work days, thank you very much."

Ken rose to his feet again.

"Ladies and gentlemen. I'll now ask the administrative staff to leave us while we discuss other policy matters. Again, my thanks to you all for coming. Perhaps the rest of us can move to be a bit closer together. We're rather too well distributed round the table for sensible discussion."

"Good luck," Poppy whispered as she

gathered her notes together. "Let me know what's going on, won't you?"

Sarah smiled and nodded. Good old Poppy. Liked to be in on everything. She would certainly pass on any bits of information she didn't consider to be confidential.

The meeting dragged on with various ideas being tossed around. Sarah was feeling uncomfortable. Her arm was hurting and there was nowhere to rest it comfortably.

Somehow, her concentration was affected and she was missing out large chunks of information. Her mind wandered round shopping lists and clients she must remember to call later. Finally, she did manage to hear that each of the more junior staff would be interviewed personally by Alex and that he would be setting fresh targets for each of the fee-earners.

Fee-earners, she grimaced. The hourly rates charged by the fee-earning solicitors were so high because all the practice expenses came out of the fees. The cost of secretaries, the offices, rates and everything else came out of what the fee earners generated.

The trouble was, most of the clients seemed to think the solicitors actually earned that much per hour and grumbled about it, compared with their own hourly rates. Now it seemed, they would be expected to charge even more. Sarah was not the only member of the group to raise eyebrows and feel some trepidation about what she was hearing.

Targets were a nightmare. It was a buzzword that was creeping in everywhere. Health service. Schools. Police. Maybe it was necessary in some ways, but targets took no notice of individuals. Made no allowance for the real human problems they all had to face each day.

She was leaving the room, intent on checking her mail in her own office when Alex caught her arm.

"It was you yesterday, wasn't it? Large stallion and an unmoveable bale of hay?"

"Yes. Thanks again for your timely help. I'm surprised you recognised me. I was certainly looking at my very worst."

"Oh, I wouldn't say that. A little tousled maybe, but still attractively vulnerable." Sarah gasped. Attractively vulnerable? What on earth did that mean? He must feel pity for her. That would never do. "Look, I meant what I said. Why don't you bring Major over to my place. I have several loose boxes and a decent paddock. Plenty of room for two. And Moonlight would enjoy the company."

"Moonlight's your mare, I take it?"

"Certainly is. She's a gorgeous girl. I'm so thrilled to have decent accommodation for her at last. My previous place had nothing and she had livery at a place several miles from me."

"You can't be too far from me, if you were riding there yesterday."

"I've bought the old Darnley place."

"What, the Manor House? Wow."

"It is rather gorgeous. Needs endless work and will undoubtedly be a huge drain on my resources, but I'm delighted with it."

Sarah couldn't help but be impressed. It was a huge old house and must have cost him a fortune. Solicitors were rarely short of money, but at his age, certainly no more than mid-thirties, how on earth could he afford it? "I had a favourite uncle leave me a considerable amount of money so I decided to put it into a decent piece of real estate," he told her, as if reading her mind.

"Very nice too. We could all do with a favourite uncle like that. Sorry, that sounded rude."

"No worries. So, do you want to stable your horse with me? You can come and see him every day. It's a bit of a long walk, but

you'll be able to drive again before too
long."

"It's very kind of you. But why would you
offer to do this for a complete stranger?"

"You may have been a stranger yesterday,
but we're working colleagues today. Besides,
I don't like to see someone struggling,
especially a pretty woman. Besides, there's
the horse to think of."

"I don't know what to say. It may be some
time before I'm really back to my normal
self." She was actually beginning to feel a
little patronised. All that stuff about her being a pretty woman. And vulnerable. How
could he think she was vulnerable? Well,
perhaps as far as her horse was concerned,
she might be a bit the worse for wear at
present. But vulnerable, she was certainly
not.

"Then say yes. If you have the worry of
your horse all the time, it could slow down
your progress. Besides, it will be nice to get
to know someone properly. I'm a complete
newcomer to the area. Apart from a beach
holiday when I was six, I've never been to
Cornwall. I've always wanted to live near
the sea and now I can. You can show me
round. Show me the best places to ride
around here. See, it's a two way thing."

"It's very kind of you . . ."

"Please stop saying that. I've told you, I shall be delighted to have company for Moonlight and someone with whom I can share a few outings. I can come round with my trailer after work, if you like. It may be a bit too far for you to lead him."

"Well, if you're sure. Thanks."

"Good. I'll see you before you leave and fix times."

Feeling slightly bemused at the speed of everything, Sarah went into the front office. Poppy pounced on her.

"I saw you talking to Mr Handsome. What's he like? Is he married? Children? Where does he live?"

"Dunno. Dunno. Dunno. Darnley Manor House."

"What, that old place near you? Very handy. So, why didn't you probe a bit? We need to know what we're up against. I mean, if there's a gorgeous Mrs Weston and a string of Junior Westons, we don't want to waste anytime, do we? Darnley Manor House, eh? That sounds like money in the family."

"Oh, an uncle left him some money and he decided to invest it in property."

"Ah, so you did do a bit of probing."

"Poppy, you are incorrigible. Now, I'm going to see if there's anything I can do to lower what Charles terms my skyscraper in-tray."

She went into her office and saw the mountain of mail on her desk. She couldn't even open the envelopes one-handed. She flicked through them and picked out a few that might be urgent. She went back into reception.

"Is anyone free for a little while? I need some help opening stuff. Hasn't anyone even looked at my mail?"

"We've been really busy," Poppy told her. "Chloe's been off as well and so we're a secretary down."

"Not really good enough. There may be clients waiting for a reply and getting upset because they haven't heard from us."

"I'm sorry, but it's been pretty chaotic. But you're right. There have been quite a few phone calls."

"Looks as if my sick leave is over. I'll be able to fend off the phone calls at least. I'll have to organise a taxi."

"I could always pick you up," said a voice from the doorway.

"Oh, Mr Weston, that's kind of you."

"It's Alex and I shall be passing your place anyway. Can't always guarantee a lift home, but half the battle's over if I bring you in.

Besides, it also ensures you're on time for work."

"I'm always . . ." she begun and noticed a smile twitching the corners of his mouth. "Once more, many thanks. It's very good of you. Now, if there's someone available to help me, Poppy, I'll go and make a start on my skyscraper."

"You're definitely in there," Poppy hissed as she passed.

"Poppy," Sarah said with a warning glare.

She returned to her office and pushed the stack of envelopes to one side. Luckily, the secretaries had phoned her clients so the appointment diary was comfortingly empty. She booted up her computer and waited. She typed in the password and saw over two hundred messages waiting for her.

"Oh no," she groaned. The trouble was, people expected a quick answer to their e-mails and never seemed to realise that it took a long time to read them and be able to make the appropriate response. It was rarely if ever, a one sentence answer to what sounded like a simple enquiry.

She glanced down the list and saw there were a large number from the same person. He was clearly impatient, despite her message saying that she was off sick and that he would be contacted as soon as possible after her return. It was a rather messy divorce case with his wife refusing to grant him access to his children.

She had heard only one-sided details from him and was concerned to discover the real reasons behind the problem. There were often many problems she didn't really want to know about, but her job demanded it. Poppy came in.

"I've got five minutes if you'd like me to open your mail. I can take the heap to my desk after opening the urgent ones and slit the rest ready for you to look at later."

"Thanks. I'd never realised how many simple tasks demand two hands."

"You look weary," she added sympathetically.

"I am. I haven't been sleeping well. Six more weeks of it. How will I ever get through it without going potty?"

"Well, now, you have the gorgeous Mr Alex Weston to console you."

"Did I hear my name?" said the man himself as he looked in at the open door. Poppy had the grace to blush.

"I was just saying that your offer to look after Sarah's horse must be a great consolation to her," she replied with a sheepish grin.

He smiled and slightly raised one eyebrow.

"I shall look forward to being both a

consolation and whatever else, to Sarah."
He turned to Sarah. "When you are finished
with whatever you're doing, can you come
into my office? I'd like to discuss things with
you and might as well see you first. I'm assuming you will be taking a few more days
off?"

"I was thinking of coming in, if only to
make calls and though I'm limited, there
are things I can do to keep the workload
under control. I can probably even reply to
some e-mails with one hand."

"Then I shall be pleased to offer you a lift
in. When you're ready . . ." He swept out of
her office and she smiled at Poppy and gave
a shrug.

"Seems like I have my orders. If you just
open whatever envelopes you have time to
do, I can look at the contents later. Thanks
for your help."

"No worries. Good luck with Mr Wonderful."

Sarah gave her a warning glance. Sometimes Poppy didn't know when to stop. A
joke was a joke, but she could take it too
far.

"Come and sit over here," Alex invited,
pointing her towards the casually arranged

comfortable armchairs away from the large desk.

"You've rearranged the office," she said. "It's nice. Much less formal. Should make the clients feel more relaxed."

"That's the idea. They are more likely to talk openly if they feel relaxed. You should try it. I expect the family law side of things is rather more stressful than any business clients."

"Well, yes, it is. Nobody comes to me unless they are deeply distressed. I spend a fortune on tissues," she tried to make a small joke.

"You shouldn't have to do that. I'll make a note to order them in. But do try the furniture move."

"Well actually, there isn't room in my office. There's just about enough space for my desk and a couple of straight back chairs for the clients. More than two people at once and it's a case of find another room."

"So we need a dedicated interview room? Something a little more casual maybe?"

"There is a small room, but it's usually booked by someone else. There's really not a room that is regularly available for us lesser mortals."

Alex was busily writing notes. He certainly seemed willing to listen and hopefully, might act on suggestions. He looked up, startled by her words.

"Lesser mortals? What do you mean by that?"

She blushed. "Well, those of us concerned with the less profitable, family law. Most of our clients are undergoing marriage break ups and access battles. They rarely have any money and the restrictions on legal support don't help them all. Sorry if I'm being too blunt for you, but the situation exists and I hope you're aware of it."

"Well, yes of course. But it doesn't mean I am able to set your target less than everyone else's."

She gave a shrug. "Set away, but if it's unrealistic, I can only do my best. Can't get blood out of stones and all that."

"I'll set what I think you should achieve and if it's not possible, you can always discuss it with me. And incidentally, I'd like to keep our private arrangements outside the office. Your horse. Lifts in etc. Both are only temporary arrangements while you are incapacitated. We can't afford any office gossip."

"Oh absolutely. The ancillary staff are inclined to make the most of absolutely anything. Nothing to do with the clients, of course. They are completely discreet and trustworthy."

"Well, I think that's about it for now. Would you like a lift home this evening?"

"If that's convenient. Then we can decide about transferring Major to your place."

"Fine. You might as well stay on for dinner after that and we can sort out some routine."

"That's very kind of you. But won't your wife mind? I mean, it's a bit short notice."

"My housekeeper will organise something. I'll call her right away."

"OK. Well, thanks very much. I appreciate it. Let me know when you're ready."

"I plan an early finish today, as it's my first day and I have so many other things to organise. I don't officially begin till next week, but there are some things I need to get out of the way. Say four o'clock? It gets dark quite early so we need to get ourselves sorted as soon as possible. I'll see you then."

"Thanks again." She left the office and went back to her own little room. A housekeeper, eh? Did that mean he was single? Interesting.

A FRIENDSHIP BEGINS TO GROW

By four o'clock, Sarah felt exhausted. Poppy had dashed out at lunchtime to buy sandwiches. She had eaten them at her desk as she read her mail and answered a few e-mails. Doing absolutely everything one-handed seemed to make every task a major effort. She was very relieved when Alex arrived to take her home.

"You look very weary. I suggest you take a few more days off before you return to full-time work. Now, if you've got everything, let's go."

Gratefully, she said goodnight to everyone and went out to the car park. Alex had a surprisingly modest car, a model similar to her own. She made no comment as she climbed in, struggling with the seat belt.

"Here, let me help." He leaned over her and took the clasp and pushed it into the socket. She was aware of a pleasant smell of aftershave, nothing too strong like the one worn by Charles. This was subtle and slightly mysterious, rather like the wearer.

"Thanks," she murmured. "It seems I can do nothing much for myself at present. I feel so useless."

"Don't be impatient. These things always

take time. You need to relax for a while and allow people to help you. It isn't a sign of feminine weakness you know."

Sarah stared at him. Was he a mind reader? She always felt the need to be extra independent so she could feel that she worked on equal terms with her male colleagues. "You'll be able to do so much more if you allow yourself time. Broken limbs can be extremely painful."

"You sound as if you speak from experience."

"When you've been riding most of your life, you usually break something or other from time to time. I used to compete. Time trials. Cross country. That sort of thing."

"Wow. I'm just an enthusiast. Oh, I did Pony Club stuff when I was a kid. I bought Major when I got my fist proper job. A long held ambition."

They chatted easily all the way to his rather magnificent home. He planned to collect his horse box and then drive back to Major's field.

"What's he like in a horse trailer?" Alex asked.

"Not the best. In fairness though, he hasn't had a lot of experience. I usually ride over to any event we're going to take part in. Local rides and so on. But he's a good boy and usually behaves well with me. Once I can get a head collar on him, he'll lead into the trailer quite well, I should think. Hope."

They arrived and he hooked up the trailer to an elderly Landrover which was standing in an open shed to one side of the house. The whole place had a slight air of neglect, but Sarah could hardly wait to see it. It was the talk of the village, the old manor house. It had been for sale for many months, since the former owner had died. She'd had no children and the beneficiaries lived abroad so selling it had seemed the only option.

"As I said, there's a massive amount of work to be done. I've made a start in the kitchen and have one habitable bedroom and bathroom. It's going to be a long job and clearly, a labour of love. Now, if you don't mind a rather bumpy ride, we'll go and collect this horse of yours."

She climbed into the Landrover with a certain amount of difficulty and they moved off. "I only keep this vehicle as a sort of mechanised wheelbarrow and for pulling the trailer. I've had it for years and can't bear to part with it. Not exactly a senior partner image, but it does the job."

"You don't present that much of a senior partner image all round," Sarah blurted out.

He looked startled. "Sorry, I didn't mean to sound rude. You seem almost too approachable and thoughtful."

"Just wait till you see me in action. Properly in action. I doubt you'll feel the same way." She sat quietly and looked out of the window. She hoped she hadn't offended him. He was being so very kind to her and the last thing she meant to do was upset him.

It was beginning to get dark by the time they reached her paddock. They hurried to get Major loaded. She collected the head collar from the stable and called him over with an apple as a bribe.

He trotted over and nuzzled her affectionately. Alex held out another apple and the stallion whinnied with pleasure. Alex took the head collar and deftly put it over the horse's head. Together, they walked him to the trailer. He was perfectly behaved and walked up the ramp without a moment of trouble.

"Wow, that was easier than I expected." Sarah remarked.

Alex smiled. "I have a way with horses."

The accommodation for the horses at Darnley consisted of three separate stone built stables, two of which had separate loose boxes inside. The straw for bedding and all the fodder and riding tack were kept in one of the other buildings. All of this led off an enclosed yard, providing a near perfect environment for horses. The paddock was across the lane that led to the house itself, so it was all extremely convenient.

It wasn't long before Major was being settled into a stable next to Moonlight. There was already a hay net hanging ready for him and straw on the floor.

"I'll give him a bucket feed, same as Moonlight, then he'll get used to me. I'll put them both out in the paddock tomorrow, assuming it isn't too cold. They'll soon get used to each other and I can see a blossoming friendship any moment. Then we'll go inside and get something hot to eat."

"I can't thank you enough. I'm sorry if I seemed reluctant to take up your offer yesterday. I just had no idea who you were."

"Don't worry about it. I'd have been the same if a stranger offered to look after my valuable horse."

Still wearing his business suit, Alex busied himself with buckets of food and water for the two stables.

His own mare was clearly delighted to see him and made affectionate little snorts. He brushed himself off as he came out of the stable.

"I always forget horses are so messy. Another job for the dry cleaners, I guess. Is there one locally?"

"I think the local garage has an agency but no, no actual dry cleaners for miles."

"Then I shall have to buy myself a boiler suit to pull over my clothes. Quickest thing during these dark evenings. Now, let's get inside and see what Mrs Harper has cooked up for us."

"Night, Major," she whispered, patting her beloved horse's neck. "See you tomorrow. And just you be on your best behaviour. Don't let me down." She bolted the door and went across the yard.

However dilapidated the rest of the out-buildings, the stable block seemed very well appointed. Alex went into the kitchen door and held it open for her. It was a delightful, farmhouse kitchen. A wide oak dresser held a range of colourful country pottery and a shelf near the cooker was stocked with cast-iron pots and dishes.

Lovely light honey coloured granite surfaces gave plenty of work space and oak cupboards suggested massive amounts of storage. Her own kitchen would have fitted into just two of the units.

43

"What a wonderful kitchen," she exclaimed. "I love the colours. The granite is a gorgeous finish and the tiles are beautiful. Lovely warm, rustic colours. And the floor too. Really easy to keep clean, I should think."

"Thanks. I'm pleased with it all. As I said, it's the only downstairs room that's been done so far. Everywhere else is a bit of a mess. I'll show you round later but right now, I'm ready for a drink. We have to eat in the kitchen, I'm afraid. Only warm place. Hope you like red wine?" He was already pulling the cork from what looked an expensively labelled bottle.

"I certainly do. Thank you. This is all a rare treat for me. But where's your Mrs er . . . Harper, wasn't it?"

"She'll have long gone. Left a casserole in the Aga, I expect." He lifted the lids of two pans on the side. "Vegetables all prepared and ready to heat."

"I could do with a Mrs Harper myself," she laughed as he handed her a glass of wine. She sniffed it and recognised a quality aroma.

"Good girl. I'm pleased you didn't just swig it down. It's a rather nice claret. One of my favourites."

"I should think not. My father would

44

never approve of that. I'm no expert but I do enjoy a nice bottle of wine."

He put boiling water into the vegetables and set them on the Aga. She sat at the oak table and watched as Alex put out cutlery and table mats. He was clearly used to fending for himself, as much as he had to.

They chatted easily and she realised just how much she was enjoying his company. She discovered he had never been married. He had concentrated on building his career and spent very little time enjoying life, by his own admission.

"That's all going to change now. I'm planning a total lifestyle change. Moving to Cornwall and finding this place was a bonus after finding the practice vacancy. I have to confess to knowing Ken. He was once a colleague of my father's. They were at university together and remained in touch over the years. After my father died, he helped my mother sort out the estate. I was overseas at the time and couldn't get out of my contract immediately."

"So, where does your mother live?"

"Devon. Just outside Exeter. Near enough for me to help her when needed and far enough away not to be in each other's way."

"I know just what you mean. My parents are near Launceston so the same thing applies. My sister lives near them. Handy for babysitting. Beth has three children."

"And what about you? No fiancé or boyfriend in tow?"

"Like you, I've concentrated on my career. I've been out with a few local men from time to time but nobody is special in my life."

"Sad pair, aren't we?"

"I disagree. I love my work and always have plenty to do."

"I must serve dinner before the vegetables are inedible." He was efficient and clearly, very competent. He lifted the lid of the casserole and sniffed appreciatively. "Hope you're not vegetarian. I didn't think to ask. This is one of Mrs Harper's special game casseroles."

"Smells wonderful."

He served a generous plate of the meat and vegetables and put it on her table mat. "I asked her not to put in any bones so it should be easy to eat one-handed."

"You're very thoughtful, Alex. Thank you." He seemed too good to be true, she thought as she waited for him to sit beside her. She dug her fork into a piece of meat and closed her eyes as the flavour hit her taste buds. "Mmm! That is just heavenly. And wonderful to have someone cook for me. The best I've managed is a microwave meal and some fresh salads."

When they had finished, he took her on his promised tour of the house. As he had said, it was in a very poor state of repair in places. Basically, it was a sound building and much of the deterioration was a matter of re-plastering and decoration.

"Wow, this is going to be a fantastic room," Sarah exclaimed as they went into the lounge. There were five tall windows along one side and two smaller windows each side of the room. "It must be a very light room with so many windows. What are the views like?"

"There's a distant sea view from one side. The other side is dominated by trees, but I plan to get them cut back a little. It's all very overgrown and neglected." Sarah gave a shiver. "Come on. Let's get back into the warm. I'll make some coffee and then if you don't mind, I'll drive you home. I know it's only eight-thirty but I have some work to do and an early start tomorrow."

"That's no problem. I was up early this morning to get into work on time. I'm feeling shattered. But thank you so much for everything. You've been incredibly kind and I'm sure Major is in very good hands."

"No problem. I'll give you a call at the

weekend and see if you are ready to start back next week. I expect you'd also like to come over some time to visit Major. Come whenever you like, if you can get transport organised."

"Thank you again. I may come over during the day later in the week."

Alex drove her home and left her at her door. The cottage looked so tiny after his magnificent place. But, it was home and hers.

She put on the television and settled down to watch something simple and mindless. It was company rather than anything, something to have buzzing away in the background while she thought about the new man in the office. It was going to be interesting working with him . . . besides anything else that might happen outside the office. He was clearly prepared to be a friend and had intimated that he would enjoy sharing her passion for riding.

The following day seemed rather dreary without having to look after Major. She wanted to allow him time to settle and besides, it meant asking a favour from someone, to drive her over to Alex's place. It was just too daunting a distance to walk there.

She read through some of the office mail she had brought home and sorted it into various piles. She could make some phone calls to respond to a few of the letters but that would need confirmation by letter as well, so there was little point in wasting her time.

She put the television on, made a cup of tea and was soon immersed in the decision of a couple choosing to live in the country or town. It was amazingly compulsive, this daytime television. But, she really needed to be back at work. This was all too different a lifestyle and she was bored. She would phone Alex that evening and ask for a lift to work the following day, besides, it was an excuse to ask after Major. She grilled some bacon and thought how much nicer the previous evening's meal had been.

Sarah's phone rang at six o'clock. She did not recognise the number.

"Hi Sarah. It's Alex. I'm almost passing your place. Thought you might like to offer me a glass of wine or something?"

"Yes, of course. Come right in."

"With you in two minutes."

She put the phone down and panicked. Had she got a decent bottle of wine any-where? The place was a mess. She was a mess. Two minutes he'd said. Barely time to even comb her hair. She finger brushed it and glanced in the mirror. Nothing she could do about it.

She scrambled into the cupboard and found a bottle of wine her father had given her recently. That must be all right. She couldn't manage to open it to allow it to breathe. Glasses. Decent glasses. She pulled two from the cupboard and wiped them as best she could. The doorbell rang. Can't have been two minutes, she thought.

"Hi. Welcome. Sorry I'm a mess. Do come in."

"Thanks. This is very cosy. I like the way you've arranged everything."

"Thank you. Not quite up to the grandeur of your place, but it's home. Some of it is even my own. I'm afraid you'll have to pull the cork." She handed him the bottle and corkscrew.

"Do you mean to say you've been unable to open a bottle of wine for the whole week?"

"True, but I'm no solitary drinker. Haven't really thought about it." She watched as he deftly opened the wine. He sniffed the cork and nodded his approval and poured two glasses. "Oh, I may have some nibbles somewhere. Hang on." She scrabbled in the cupboard and found some packets of savouries and handed them to him to open. "I'm pretty useless, aren't I?"

"I wondered if you're doing anything at the weekend? Saturday to be exact."

"No. Saturday is usually my day for a long ride. But, I won't be doing that for a little while. Why?"

"I'm going to look at some pups. Black labs. I wondered if you'd like to come along? They won't be ready for another couple of weeks, but I've been planning an addition to the family for some time. This seems like the right thing to do at this stage. Mrs Harper is evidently devoted to dogs so will be pleased to look after it during the day. She's there every day, supervising the workmen, so a dog won't be lonely."

"I'd love to. Thanks for asking me. I adore Labradors too. We always had them when I was a child."

"Them?"

"Yes. Two of them. Sisters. One each for me and my sister, though in reality they were both my mother's. We always thought two together were company for each other as well."

"That's a thought, perhaps I should consider getting a pair." He emptied his glass and stood up. "Thanks very much for that. I'll look forward to seeing you on Saturday.

51

I must go and sort out the horses. Mrs H was putting them into the stables before she left."

"Your Mrs Harper sounds like a dream. Supervising workmen. Cooking meals. Devoted to dogs. Better than any wife. She must be younger than I thought."

"She's about thirty. A widow. Tragic story. Her husband was killed in a motoring accident. She needed work so it's all very convenient. No children and her time's her own. And she lives quite close by."

"That's great for both of you. Actually, I was thinking of coming into the office tomorrow. I'm bored here and there's plenty I could do. Would you be able to pick me up in the morning?"

"Certainly, if you're sure you're ready to return. Eight o'clock suit you?"

"That's fine," Sarah replied with a slight gulp. It was a bit early but she didn't have to see to Major. "Thanks very much. I'll organise a taxi home when I've had enough."

She watched him drive away. This was the start of something, she was certain.

Alex Tries To Impress The Staff

Promptly at two minutes to eight the next morning, Alex stopped outside her cottage and sounded his horn. Sarah was ready and waiting and carefully locked the door.

"Good morning. Thank you for this," she said in the same friendly tone as she had said goodbye the previous evening.

"No Problem. Glad you were ready on time. I'm afraid I can be rather impatient where work days are concerned."

"How's Major this morning?"

"He's fine. Seems to have settled." He was silent as he concentrated on driving through the early traffic when they reached Truro. She kept quiet too, sensing that he didn't want small talk.

He pulled into the small car park and into a space that she noticed now carried a sign with his name on it. Surely an indication that he was certainly a presence within the firm. "Right," he said briskly. "I'll see you during the day at some point. We need to discuss a number of things. Don't feel obliged to work the full day if you get tired. Take a taxi home. You can charge it to the firm, under these special circumstances."

"Well, that's very kind of you. Thanks.

Hopefully, I shall be able to work my usual hours, even if I need a bit of extra help with some things."

"Excellent. See you later." He strode off into the building, not waiting for her to catch up or even to hold the door open for her. She shrugged. Maybe he didn't want anyone to notice that he had given her a lift, not that anyone significant would be in the building this early.

Some of the other partners came in early, but the receptionist and secretaries rarely arrived much before nine o'clock. There were clearly two sides to Alex Weston and home and work did not mix. That was fine by her. She opened her office door and settled down in front of a new heap of mail. Poppy had carefully slit open the envelopes and left them ready for her return. How thoughtful, she smiled to herself.

As the staff arrived, several of them waved or called greetings through the door. Every-one seemed pleased to see her and she felt the warm glow of being wanted.

By the end of the morning, Sarah had completely forgotten that she had ever been away. She had a small digital recorder and made great use of it, instead of making her usual written notes for the secretaries to type her letters.

She made lots of calls and set up appointments for clients for the following day. She would need to read up some files during the evening so she was completely up to date with everything. There was one particularly difficult case where she was acting for the father, following a messy divorce. The ex-wife was claiming that his child was unwilling to see him and he was very distressed.

On the wife's instructions, she needed to arrange supervised access through social services and somehow, to persuade his ex to allow it and comply with the divorce agreement. She hated such cases where feelings were running so high, knowing logic and common sense got lost in the welter of emotions that had killed what had once been love. It had made Sarah herself very cautious about her own life. She often wished she could have been as certain as her sister.

When Beth and Mike had decided to marry, it had always been exactly what they both wanted and neither of them had any doubts. Neither of them had ever had any other person in their lives and they both seemed just as happy now after all the years. Maybe she had simply not met the right person and when she did, there would be no worries. Meantime, she had to try to sort out the complexities of Mr Knowles and his family.

It was almost five o'clock when Sarah realised that she hadn't had her meeting with Alex. Too late now, she decided and tidied her desk, ready to call a taxi and go home. Her phone rang.

"Miss Pennyweather? Sarah. Mr Weston wonders if it would be convenient to see him now?" It was Julia, his secretary, an elderly lady who had been with the company for many years. She had previously worked exclusively for Ken, the now retiring head of the practice. She wondered what Julia thought of her new boss, the new head of practice in all but name.

"Fine," she murmured, mentally cancelling her relatively early finish. "I'll come along right away." She picked up her briefcase and pushed various documents into it for reading at home. She felt weary but there was only one more day before the weekend.

She had a little thrill as she thought of going out on Saturday to look at puppies with Alex. Maybe they could stop at some nice country pub on the way back. Thoughts of log fires and cheery warm bar food seemed most appealing. She wondered if she dare mention it to him.

"Mr Weston is waiting for you," Julia said as she arrived in the outer office. "Go straight in. Would you like anything to drink? Tea, coffee, water?"

"No thanks. I'm going straight home when I finish here. I'll use your phone afterwards if you don't mind. I need to call a taxi as I can't drive yet."

"I'd offer to do it for you but I don't know how long you'll be and I'm about to leave for the day."

"Thanks. No problems." She tapped on the door and walked in without waiting for a reply.

"Good evening. Hope you had a good day? Thanks for coming in. Hope it hasn't made you late for anything?"

"No. I was about to call a taxi so you caught me at the right moment." He indicated a seat and she sat down.

"I've been working on everyone's targets, today. We need to revise the whole system if we are to keep all the administrative staff. Business rates are rising and well, frankly, there just isn't enough income being generated." He handed her a sheet of paper. "This is what I've set for you, based on the client base you had over the past six months and your own fee hours."

She glanced down at the words and figures

and gasped. She looked back at him. "You are surely joking? I can't achieve this. For one thing, it depends on who walks in through the door. You've seen the sort of cases I work on. As I said the other day, these are all people with little or no income. They've been through divorces and a family break up. Some of them are struggling to pay unrealistic fees set by the support agency. How can I suddenly start charging them fees like this?"

The cool grey eyes stared back at her, unblinking. He was silent. The mouth she had thought generous and attractive was set in a firm line. He drew in his breath at last, he spoke.

"I'm sorry you see it that way. I'm really not trying to be unreasonable but we have to face reality. It's a case of this or sack two or more of the admin staff. I know none of you would be happy with that. We all rely on them for many things and you'd end up doing things like your own photocopying and typing letters. That strikes me as being a waste of expensive time and inevitably would mean longer hours. Give it a try and we'll review it in a few weeks. Now, I mustn't keep you any longer. You'll be wanting to get home."

"Right. Thanks. Erm, would it be convenient for a lift in tomorrow?"

"Certainly. Same time as this morning?"

"Thanks. That's fine." She hesitated, wondering when he'd have time to see to Major and his own horse. It didn't look as though he was ready to leave yet and it was already dark outside. Her horse would need his feed and to be put inside the stable.

"Is there something else? I'm afraid I'm not finished yet so I can't offer you a lift home."

"No, it wasn't that. I was . . ."

"Oh. You're worried about Major? It's fine. Mrs Harper was putting them both in the stables and seeing to the feed for both of them. They'll be well looked after. No worries."

"Thank you," she murmured. Good old Mrs Harper, she thought sarcastically. The woman was obviously making herself indispensable. So what, she thought. She should be grateful someone was looking after her dear Major. Why should she feel any sort of silly resentment, or could it be jealousy, about the woman.

Alex may have been friendly enough outside work, but he certainly wasn't showing her any favours in the office. In fact, she would be interested to see if everyone had such unrealistic targets set or whether he was actually making sure he wasn't seen to be showing her any favouritism. She tried to convince herself that he was nothing to her on a personal level.

It was kind of him to take in her horse and to have given her a meal the other night, but whatever her idiotic thoughts might have been the previous evening, they didn't have a future and it wasn't the start of something. She dialled the taxi firm and went into the reception area to wait. Alex Weston was an enigma.

"I'm so glad it's Friday," called Charles Talbot as he breezed through reception the next day. "I do love Fridays. My, you are getting in early these days," he said as he leaned on the door post of Sarah's office. She and Alex had driven in with very few words again. He wasn't a man who liked to chatter when driving, she had realised.

"Lots to catch up on." She could smell his aftershave from the other side of the room. Someone should tell him about it, she thought.

"Trying to impress, are we?"

"Not at all." He was on a fishing trip, try-ing to find out if there was anything going on between her and Alex. Perhaps Poppy had been talking out of place.

"Look, can I have a word?" He came into

the office and closed the door. "I was wondering if his majesty had given you his idea of what targets are possible?"

"Well, yes."

"And?" He raised his eyebrows. "And are yours remotely achievable?"

"Actually, no. At least most of your work is property based. Mine is all the family stuff that simply doesn't pay because nobody can afford it."

"You must know what the property market is like these days. Everything's seizing up. I don't have a hope of getting even half way there."

"Well, at least I know it isn't just me he's singled out for a boost in keeping the company afloat."

"So what are we going to do about it?"

"He told me to see how it goes for a few weeks and then we can meet again to discuss it."

"I'm not happy about it. Not one bit."

"Nor me, but there's nothing else to do. We can't be responsible for half the staff being sacked. Now, you must excuse me. I have a client coming in half an hour and I need to refresh myself on his notes."

"Fancy a drink after work? Friday night treat?"

"Sorry, no. I can't."

"Shame. So, who's the new guy in your life?"

"There's no new guy," she snapped, blushing.

"Don't give me that. Someone's putting a blush on your cheeks and a spring in your step."

"There's nobody, I assure you."

"Great. That means there might still be hope for yours truly. And if you change your mind about that drink . . . give me a buzz."

She shook her head as she pulled out her notes and settled to work.

It was a difficult morning. She felt so sorry for her first client and did what she could to comfort him. She agreed to speak to his ex-wife's solicitor and see what could be arranged. The worst part came when she informed of their increased charges. His face fell and he looked distraught.

"But I can't afford that much. Does that mean I can't have you working for me any more?"

"I'll do whatever I can, I promise you. It's all out of my hands. You must understand the economic climate is a problem for all of us. Leave it with me. I'm sure I can find ways to prune what I have to charge."

She showed him out. Along with the wretched targets, there was a time sheet where she was supposed to write down pretty much every bit of work she was doing for every minute of her day.

It was supposed to be a temporary thing, so the powers-that-be could have more idea of how time was being managed. None of it took account of the fact that she often spent her lunchtimes at her desk working, while she munched her sandwiches. Getting in early and leaving late were also a part of her usual routine and none of this was being taken into consideration, it seemed to her. Speaking to the other juniors over coffee, she sensed a feeling of rebellion brewing. Alex was not making himself popular right from the start of his tenure.

Charles was leading the debate.

"I mean to say, how can we actually charge extra when the clients aren't coming into the office in the first place. We can hardly go and drag them in off the street. I was even thinking of going round to the estate agents and getting them to recommend me, assuming they ever manage to make a sale in the first place."

"You can't do that. It isn't legal."

"I know. But desperate times . . ."

There was a great sense of unrest in what had previously been a happy practice. Sarah felt embarrassed about seeing Alex outside work, largely because he was taking the brunt of everyone's dissatisfaction. She returned to her office and began to answer some e-mails, her one handed typing improving sufficiently to make it a practical task. Charles came into her office once more.

"If you intend trying to persuade me to go out with you . . ." she began.

"Not this time. You seem to be closer than most to the new broom. Any chance you might talk to him? I think he's going to have open rebellion on his hands if he doesn't see reason."

"I'm not actually that close," she said flatly. "I've simply been having a couple of lifts into work, while I can't drive. He says absolutely nothing when we're driving and makes it clear he won't discuss office politics with me. I have been thinking about the situation though. I'm really wondering if the problem rests with the past and the kindly Ken. Maybe he never wanted to rock any boats and the whole system has been slowly collapsing. The credit crunch has just made everything so much more urgent."

"Someone said you'd defend him. Clearly you do have some sort of relationship burgeoning. Sorry I bothered you."

"For goodness sake, Charles. It's nothing

like that. There is no relationship. I'm not defending him. I told him my target was unreasonable and exactly why I think so."

Charles gave a snort. "And where is your precious horse at present?" She looked down. "Poppy let it slip that he was looking after him. Very cosy."

"I assure you, it means nothing. It's only while I have this dratted plaster cast on my arm. Alex happens to have a horse of his own and plenty of space to stable a second horse. Major will be back in his paddock as soon as I can manage him again. I wouldn't have put you down as an office gossip." She was angry now.

"OK. You needn't explode. I've obviously touched a sensitive area."

She sighed. What was the point? There was nothing she could say to change his opinion.

"Think what you like. There is nothing going on, but if you want to disbelieve me, that's up to you. Now, if you'll excuse me, I have another client due any moment."

He left her office, a smirk on his face. One thing that was for certain, she would not be going to look at pups with Alex the next day. It would be sure to get back to the office gossips who were determined to pair them off. It seemed that even if she had thought that she and Alex might become good friends, it was not going to be possible. He would be furious if he knew people were already talking about them.

"We're all going round to the wine bar after work," Poppy announced near the end of the day. "You will come, won't you?"

"I've already told Charles I wouldn't go out for a drink with him. So, in honesty, I really can't."

"Don't worry about him. I'll tell him I bullied you into it."

"OK then. It would be nice. I've hardly been out anywhere since my accident."

"Great. I'll give you a shout when we're ready."

Sarah tidied her desk and decided she'd done enough for the day. She completed the dreaded time sheet and dropped it into the main admin office as instructed. As she was coming out, Alex bumped into her.

"Oh, Sarah. Glad we bumped into each other. I was wondering if we might go for a quick drink before heading back to the village. Actually, I rather wanted to invite everyone to celebrate the end of my first week. What do you think?"

"Tricky one. I've just agreed to go to the wine bar with them. I'm not sure who's going. Maybe you could suggest it to the others. If it comes from me, it would look bad.

As if we had something between us."

"And we don't?"

"I don't think so."

"Pity. I thought we were getting on rather well."

"Outside the office maybe there is something. But you've hardly been Mr Popular here at work and positively cool to me."

"Then an invitation to free drinks all round might be just the thing. Who's the best one to speak to?"

"You could try Poppy, but don't let her think I put you up to it."

He gave her hand a quick squeeze and said thanks. She slipped back to her own office unnoticed, overhearing him inviting everyone to join him for a drink.

"Thanks," she heard Poppy's voice. "We're going to the Jug and Bottle. Join us there."

"Right. Half-an-hour?"

"Fine." There was a buzz of conversation as he left. Undoubtedly, the others were scolding Poppy for letting him join them.

"He is the enemy, after all," Charles was mouthing off.

"Well, it's a free drink and maybe he'll stop being the enemy if we socialise a bit."

Out of the office, Alex turned out to be quite a hit. He relaxed completely and was entertaining, charming and quite the perfect host. He bought several bottles of wine and wouldn't let any of the staff pay for their share.

Sarah watched him carefully and saw that he didn't drink more than one small glass himself, knowing he had to drive home. She was relieved to see it. Charles on the other hand, was drinking rather excessively and she knew he had a car parked back at the office.

"I hope you don't plan to drive home," she muttered to him as discreetly as possible.

"Course not. I shall take a taxi," he replied rather too loudly. "Perhaps someone would like to share my cab with me? We could have a bite to eat first and make a night of it. Any takers?" There was a sudden silence and people began to collect things together to leave, mumbling that they needed to get home.

Alex touched her shoulder and she swung round. She had been sitting at the opposite side of the table, trying to ensure nobody would make any comments.

"I might as well drop you off on my way past. It seems silly for you to order a cab."

"Well, yes. Thank you. That would be very kind."

"I'll meet you back in the office car park.

Better to be discreet."

"OK. Thanks. We don't want anyone thinking we might be friends, do we?" There was a hint of sarcasm in her tone. He glared at her and then smiled. She said her good-byes to the others and watched as they made their way home. Charles was still standing on the pavement.

"Won't you change your mind and come for something to eat? There's that nice Italian just round the corner. I shall be sober once I've eaten and I can drive you home."

"No thanks, Charles. Like I said, I need to get back home. I have a taxi coming for me at the office. See you on Monday. Have a good weekend."

"Thanks, you too," he muttered and wandered down the road. When she was sure he was out of sight, she went round the back of the offices and met Alex, sitting in his car, waiting for her.

"Sorry. Charles was being Charles and wouldn't take no for an answer. I fibbed and said I had a taxi waiting."

"That's all right. I don't mind waiting this end of the day. Are you implying that people are gossiping about us?"

"Well, yes. The fact you've been driving me into work and you also have my horse in your stables. I'm afraid Poppy overheard us making the arrangements. I can assure you, I have said nothing to encourage this office chatter. In fact I have denied everything. Not that it was difficult. You're not exactly friendly at work."

"I'm sorry. I don't mean to be unfriendly. I just get swept along with the tasks in hand. I rarely allow myself time to chat."

"Perhaps you should. You'd get a feel for what's going on."

He slowed down and looked at her. He gave a sigh. "It's Friday night. The week is over. It's been a heavy time for me. I need to relax now and forget about work. What are you doing about supper this evening?"

"Haven't really thought. Warm something up from the freezer I expect."

"Doesn't sound too exciting. What's the village pub like? We could grab something quick."

She considered the idea. "It's pretty basic. I'm not sure it's up to your gourmet standards." Without saying another word, he drove into the car park and switched off the engine. Sarah gave him a small grin and tried to unfasten her seat belt, reaching round awkwardly with her good arm. He leaned over at the same moment and their heads were close.

"Here, let me." For one mad moment, she

thought he was going to kiss her but it passed and he unfastened his own belt. Her heart had begun to beat rather rapidly and she realised she felt slightly disappointed. She quickly got out of the car and shivered in the chilly night air. He opened the door of the Lounge Bar and ushered her in.

The landlord greeted them and they ordered drinks and sat down with the menu.

"Chips with everything, it seems."

"I like chips," Sarah retorted. "Don't eat them often but they are particularly good here. I'll go for fish and chips, I think. Nice and indulgent for a Friday night."

"I'll have the same. I assume it's fresh fish not frozen catering company fish?"

She shook her head. It was usually delicious with a home-made batter and a rare treat for her. They avoided all talk of work and she learned a little more about his background. His mother lived alone, having been widowed several years earlier. She sounded quite a demanding lady. "We always called her the Duchess."

"We?"

"Dad and me. I'm an only child. My late uncle, who left me the money, had no children of his own. Seems our family don't go in for many children. If ever I manage to find anyone who'll be willing to marry me, I want lots of kids. I'd like to experience proper family life."

"Hence the gorgeous Darnley Manor. That would make a fabulous family home."

"I hope so. My mother's the only problem. Once it's all finished, I have a horrible feeling she's going to expect to come and live with me. We'd drive each other mad in no time flat. I say, this fish is excellent. Anyway, are you still willing to come and look at puppies with me tomorrow? I need to take Moonlight out in the morning, but thought we could set off in the afternoon. They're in a little village somewhere in mid Cornwall."

"I'm not sure it's a good idea if we see too much of each other. Makes our working relationship a bit tricky." She bit her lip as she spoke. She didn't mean a word of it, but knew how anxious he was to keep things separate.

"I can handle it if you can. I'd be very disappointed if you dropped out. I was looking forward to your company. And your expert eye on black labs. You said you had one as a child so you must know a bit about what to look for."

"Well, yes. I can't do much in the way of entertaining myself. I'd love to come but you know what I said about the gossips. They've already asked me to have a private word with you about the wretched targets. Seem to think I can persuade you to reconsider."

"If they want to complain, I expect them to come to me direct. Not use you as a go-between. I expect Charles was the ringleader in that little rebellion. I'm right, aren't I?"

She looked unhappy. Whatever she thought of Charles, he was a colleague and she had a strong sense of loyalty. "I don't like that young man. He's devious and I suspect, not averse to certain malpractices. But I'm only guessing and I don't expect you to break any confidences. That's enough of that. Work is banned when we're out together. Now, about tomorrow?"

"OK. But if you don't mind, I'd like to come over and see Major at some point. I'll see if someone will give me a lift during the morning. You don't need to wait for me. Go for your ride and I'll spend some time with Major and see you after lunch."

"Fine. We could have a snack if you want to wait for me. Then you'll only need one lift. Now, can I tempt you to some pudding?"

"I don't think so. I'd like to get back now. I'm feeling shattered. It's been a long day. One-armed working seems much more tiring."

Sarah sat down to watch the news on television. It seemed a very long time since she had set out that morning. It had been an interesting day. She pulled a notepad towards her and wrote left-handedly, *Contact Mrs Knowles' solicitor first thing Monday.* She could barely read it, but hopefully, it was enough to jog her memory.

Sarah Falls For Alex

Major was as delighted to see Sarah as she was to see him the next morning. Joe, her friend who had rescued her after the accident, had given her a lift over. He had been impressed that she was actually visiting Darnley Manor and even more so when he heard Major was stabled there.

She had a pocket full of apples for her beloved horse and they stood together, communing as only a horse and its rider can. He hung his great head over her shoulder and nuzzled her. She patted him with her good arm and fed him yet another apple.

"You're a totally cupboard loving animal," she told him fondly. "Stomach driven, aren't you?" He whinnied and looked round. She saw Alex and Moonlight riding past the hedge and Major started to move towards them. Clearly the stallion was already besotted with the mare.

He ignored Sarah and went to stand by the gate, waiting for Alex to unsaddle his horse and brush her down. She should have brought her own grooming kit and worked on Major. But then, he was still wearing his horse rug so she couldn't possibly have managed it one handed.

"Had a good ride?" Sarah asked as she leaned over the yard gate.

"Not bad. I shall look forward to us being able to ride together. There's a nice bridle path round the edge of the land and a couple of gallops at the far end. Is there a way down to the beach anywhere?"

"Yes, if you go along the road for a little way. Seems Major has already formed an attachment for Moonlight. He was welcoming you back when he saw you. Totally forgot about me."

"I heard him. Moonlight's pretty keen too. She's most anxious to get back into the paddock. There you go, girl." He fastened the straps on the rug and led her back towards the gate. Sarah opened it and followed him back to the paddock. Major was waiting by the gate and the pair galloped round the field together, enjoying the autumn sunshine. "Shall we go and get something to eat?"

"Thanks. We seem to spend all our time eating when we're together."

"I like social eating. Food always tastes better in company. Once you've got your arm back, you can cook for me."

"Oh dear. I'm no cook. Your Mrs Harper puts me to shame. I blame my mother. She's a first rate cook and never let me do any when I was a kid. Always shoved me out of the kitchen to do my homework. I was considered the clever one and as such, shouldn't waste my time on boring chores. I never minded of course, but I do realise she wasn't really doing me any favours. Beth, my sister, is also a good cook. She was allowed to help in the kitchen."

"But she didn't have a career."

"No, but she's a terrific mum. Think I'd be pretty useless."

"You'll have to marry a wealthy man who can provide you with a cook and a nanny."

"Doubt I'd find anyone like that in this part of the world. And besides, I couldn't bear to leave Cornwall so it would have to be someone close to here." Alex remained silent and she blushed. What on earth was she thinking of, speaking so personally to her boss? But, he wasn't her boss outside work, was he? She hoped that he didn't think she was hinting in any way.

"I've got some fresh bread, cheese and paté. And some salad. Hope that will do for you."

"Excellent. So, tell me about these puppies. How old are they?"

"Eight weeks. So they are really ready to leave the mother. I didn't plan to bring it home today as I'm not really prepared for it. I thought they'd agree to keep it for me for another week to give me time to get everything set up here. There is an enclosed yard at the back and if the pup lives in the scullery during the time I'm not here, it should be fine."

"You do work rather long hours for having a dog. They need company as well as a warm place. They are easily bored if they're not exercised regularly."

"Mrs Harper is willing to take charge."

"What a treasure is Mrs Harper," Sarah said peevishly.

"You know, if I knew you better I might think you're jealous of Mrs Harper. She's a kindly soul who needs the wages I pay her."

"I'm sorry. I suppose she just makes me feel inadequate. She's good with horses and dogs. A superb cook and keeps the house beautifully. Altogether, she's everything I'm not."

"Good job I'm not paying you to look

after the house then, isn't it?"

They stacked the dishwasher and set off to find the kennels. It was an hour's drive and right in the middle of the country. The owner was a rather hearty lady who insisted on asking endless questions to make sure her pup was going to the right home.

Alex was beginning to think he should have brought his CV and a dozen references. When asked if he worked away from home, and she discovered that he and Sarah weren't married, they began to think they were being sent packing. Sarah got a fit of the giggles and had to turn away.

"Do you think we could actually see the pups?" Alex asked. The woman sniffed and led them through a kitchen, into a scullery that smelt very strongly of puppies and dog, a mixture that wasn't entirely pleasant. The yapping was intense as the puppies all clambered up the fence that separated them from the main part of the room.

Alex bent and picked up a tiny squirming bundle. He handed the pup to Sarah who cuddled it close, making small comfort noises to it. It settled with her quickly and snuggled into the crook of her arm.

"It likes you," Alex said with a grin. The one he had picked up was wriggling madly.

"They all have their own little characters.

Now, if you really want two, I shall need a deposit from you. In case you change your mind and I have then missed another sale," the owner said.

"Fair enough." He drew out a cheque book. "How much are they?" She named the price and he gasped slightly.

"They are thoroughbreds. I'll show you the pedigree. And they are wormed and fully inoculated. Are you sure you're aware of what you're doing? I don't want to let my babies go to somewhere where they won't be looked after properly."

"They'll be fine. I promise, I'll read everything I can find on what to do with pups. And Sarah and Mrs Harper between them will keep me fully in line, I'm sure."

The woman sniffed and looked at his cheque. It seemed that the promise of a sale was slightly the winner.

"Great. I'll be back next Saturday morning to collect them, complete with dog carrier. By then, I'll be fully ready to house them properly."

As Sarah and Alex drove back, both of them laughed about their experience.

"You should have asked for a bulk discount," Sarah chuckled. "I noticed her precious babies were less precious when she thought you might drop out of the deal."

"You think I've been silly? Paying over the odds?"

"Not really. They are dear little things and the mother and father both seemed to have a good temperament. I'm sure you'll be pleased with them. Besides, once you mentioned Darnley Manor as their potential home, she was positively purring."

"Snob! She doesn't know the state of it. Which reminds me, I'd like your thoughts on decor for the lounge at home. Any ideas?"

"Me? I'm not exactly up on interior design." She felt flattered that he would even consider asking her. "I'd like to see it in daylight, I must admit. It's such a gorgeous room."

"That's why I asked you. You seemed keen on it and I thought you might make some suggestions. That's my next project. Why don't you come over tomorrow?"

"You must have other things to do. I'm sure you must have seen enough of me this week."

"I'm sorry. I realise you must have other things to do. I've been taking up too much of your time. Sorry. I just get carried away with my own enthusiasms and forget that people have lives of their own. I'm afraid you'll find I'm a bit like that where work is concerned. You must tell me when I'm imposing on you."

"Would that be in or out of work?"

He said nothing and the corners of his mouth twitched as he tried to stifle a grin.

"I'll leave you to your own devices this evening. Thanks very much for your company this afternoon. I hope I haven't imposed too much. And if you do decide you'd like to visit Major tomorrow, I shall be cooking a roast at lunchtime. You could take a look at my interior design problems at the same time. But this is not a command. Come only if you'd like to."

He stopped outside her cottage and she climbed out of his car. She didn't give him an answer about the following day. Of course she wanted to spend the day with this gorgeous man, but she sensed it wasn't a good idea and simply thanked him for the outing and lunch.

Sarah watched him drive away and raised her good arm to wave. She would never know that he was watching her. She could not know that he was looking in his rear view mirror, cursing himself for being too pushy. In his own bull-in-a-china-shop way, he'd scared her off. Someone, he felt, who could be so right for him. Easily an intel-

81

lectual equal, she shared everything he held dear.

He must somehow back off and not rush her. Stop trying to thrust her into something she needed time to acknowledge. All the same, he hoped she might come over to look at her beloved horse the next morning. She did not.

Alex might have been consoled if he had known that she was pacing up and down her little garden, desperately wondering what to do. She wanted to go over to the gorgeous house and see Major. Alex was also a huge draw to her. But she had to work with him all week.

He had ideas that professionally, she did not like nor agree to follow. It could only lead to conflict in the workplace and that, she would hate. She loved her work and found pleasure in helping people, often desperate people, to come to some sort of solution in their lives. Ken had understood. He would always recognise that she would try to mediate rather than insist on her clients taking the often expensive route to litigation.

She would talk to them, advise them and try to show them they might find a solution. She spent longer than the time they were entitled to and charged them the lowest fees possible. It may not be good for business and the practice, but she was dealing with people's lives.

That was surely more important than making already well-paid lawyers even better off? She could see trouble ahead and needed time to sort out her own thoughts before becoming too involved with her ambitious new boss. All the same, Alex Weston had done something to her own emotional stability.

Roast dinner with Alex . . . or a lonely omelette? No contest really but she chose the omelette, totally based on political reasons. Towards evening, she realised they had made no arrangements for Alex to collect her for work the next day so she called him. There was no reply. She left a message and hoped he would find it.

Rather nervously the next morning, Sarah looked through her window, hoping to see Alex's car coming along the road. At five past eight, she decided she must call for a taxi. She was on the point of dialling when she heard his car stop. She put down the phone and rushed out.

"Shouldn't you lock your door?" Alex asked.

"It's OK. Locks automatically. Thanks for

stopping. I wasn't sure if you'd got my message."

"Of course. Sorry . . . I should have called back. I was out with the horses. It turned rather cold last night so I thought I should make sure they had plenty of straw."

"Thanks. I appreciate your efforts."

They made slightly polite, stilted conversation throughout the journey. The easy closeness of Saturday had gone. Sarah cursed herself inwardly. She had spent a miserable day yesterday, almost as if she was punishing herself for allowing her guard to slip and tell him too many personal things. She had missed out on his company and possibly spoilt any chance of a good future friendship or even more. He parked the car and commented,

"Another week at the grindstone. Have a good day."

They saw little of each other during the week. Sarah saw him pass her office door a few times during the days and he collected her promptly each morning. He said nothing more about seeing her outside work and by Friday, she decided that any chance that something might have progressed between them was totally lost.

There was no suggestion of drinks after work on Friday and Sarah phoned for a taxi at the end of the day. If she had been hoping to go with him to collect the puppies the next day, she was to be disappointed. No mention of it had been made. A long boring weekend lay ahead. Maybe she should go and see her parents. But getting there was just too complicated. She would have to do a one-handed clean round the cottage and shop in the village. Very exciting.

She awoke on Saturday to the sound of her phone ringing. She sat up startled and glanced at the clock. Seven o'clock. Who on earth was phoning at this time?

"Hello," she said still feeling sleepy.

"Hi. It's me. Alex." She knew his voice instantly. "Are you still willing to come with me to collect my puppies? Sorry, I never caught up with you yesterday. I need some advice about beds and other things so thought I'd go to a pet shop first thing and then drive out to collect them. I've also taken the liberty of getting Mrs H to prepare something for supper tonight. Then you can help me to settle them in."

Sarah listened in surprise. Suddenly, her weekend wasn't looking quite so bleak.

Trying not to sound too enthusiastic, she replied, "I wasn't sure you still wanted me to come with you. But yes, being unable to drive, I'm limited in what I can do. I was planning some cleaning and then a walk into the village to collect some groceries."

"If that's what you'd rather do . . ." She could hear amusement in his tone.

"Of course I'd really rather try to push the vacuum round, one-handed. But as you've asked so nicely, I'll forgo that pleasure."

"Great. I'll pick you up at nine."

Sarah pulled her plastic bag over the plaster to protect it while she showered. She couldn't wait for it to be removed and be able to get back to normal. She had a leisurely breakfast and was ready and waiting at nine o'clock. It proved to be a fun trip. Buying everything a puppy or two could possibly need and then some, produced a mammoth bill.

"I hope it's worth it," she said with a groan when the large heap of goods were finally stacked into his car. She'd persuaded him to buy one large dog bed rather than two small ones. "They'll grow out of them in no time and they're not cheap. Besides, they've been used to sleeping in one dog heap, around their mother. And I'd use an old blanket to start with. Forget the special expensive vet bed and everything. They'll probably chew everything to begin with and they are certainly not house-trained."

It was mid afternoon by the time they arrived back with their squeaking, wriggling cargo of puppies. They were let out on the lawn where they rushed around, tumbling over each other on their ridiculously fat paws.

"Come in, little dogs. This is your new home." Alex had put down the new bed in the utility room where he planned they would be housed during the night. It had a slate floor and could be easily cleaned.

They were watching the pair, enchanted as they flopped down in exhaustion for all of one minute and then leapt up again and dashed round some more. There was a tap at the door and Mrs Harper arrived.

"Hi there. Couldn't wait to see the little dears. Oh, aren't you gorgeous?" She bent and scooped up one of the pair and cuddled it. The second one chewed at the laces on her shoes so she picked up that one as well.

Sarah watched, a slight feeling of resentment brewing. This was supposed to be hers and Alex's time to get to know the dogs. She contemplated the woman, watching her smiling at Alex as she chatted to him and the pups. She looked much younger than Sarah had expected. She was a pretty blonde with a neat figure, shown off by well fitting jeans and a T shirt. There was an easy familiarity between them which made her feel ridiculously jealous.

"What have you left us for supper?" Alex asked.

"There's a pot roast to go in the oven. In fact, if you like, I'll go and put it in now. Then it can cook slowly and be ready for you in a couple of hours. There're jacket potatoes and veg all ready for you. I'd best get off now. Leave you to your new little family. I'll see you on Monday, girls. What are you calling them by the way?"

"Haven't decided yet. That's tonight's job. Thanks very much for everything." He paused. "Look, I've had an idea. Sarah here is having problems. With her broken arm she can't properly clean her cottage. How about you go round one morning and give her a hand?"

"Sure. If you can spare me for a morning."

"Oh no, really, I couldn't possibly impose," Sarah protested. She certainly didn't want anyone going around prying on her things. "It isn't that bad. Anyway, I won't be like this for much longer."

"If you're sure. It's no trouble."

Sarah shook her head. She felt furious with Alex for even suggesting the idea. "OK then, I'll go and put your dinner in the oven. Leave me a note with the names of the pups. They'll need to get used to their names and if I don't know them, it will be difficult. Enjoy your evening," she said sounding just a little wistful.

"Do you think I should have asked her to join us?" Alex whispered when Mrs Harper left the room.

"If you like. Perhaps you could ask her and I'll go and leave and go home."

He stared at her, looking puzzled. "Why would you do that?" He opened his eyes wide and then his mouth broke into a broad grin. "Don't tell me you're jealous? My, that's encouraging. Must mean you care."

She blushed and looked down at one of the pups to cover her confusion. She was ashamed of being so foolish.

It was a cozy evening. Supper was delicious, as expected. They had wine and later went into the lounge to discuss the decorating plans. It was a completely blank canvas as he had no furniture for the room so everything could be chosen from scratch.

"I'd go for pale neutral colours for the walls and add splashes of colour with the furnishings. Once it's painted, you can choose things for each area of the room and build the complete picture with everything co-ordinated."

"You really sound as if you know what you're talking about. I'd really like it if you are involved with it all."

"I'd love it. Besides, spending someone else's money sounds ideal to me."

"Let's make some sketches and notes. What are you doing tomorrow?"

"Today's cleaning?"

"That'll keep. And you didn't do any shopping so we'll go out for lunch."

"You're on. But I'll pay for lunch. You're always feeding me. It's my turn."

"An independent woman. What more could I ask?"

SARAH MEETS ALEX'S MOTHER

Despite their growing friendship out of work, over the next weeks Alex treated Sarah just as he treated the rest of the staff. Never could he be accused of favouritism.

At last, her plaster cast had been removed and she had a smaller, support splint which she could take off whenever she wanted to. She could also drive again and so ceased her morning drives with Alex. At least the office gossip about them had been dropped. They did see a lot of each other outside work. She had left Major staying at Darnley

Manor and Alex had even suggested she stop renting her own paddock and leave him there permanently.

It was however, a step too far in her estimation. She agreed her horse was better placed there for the harsher winter months. Another couple of weeks, it would be Christmas.

She wondered what Alex would be doing for the holiday. Her parents were expecting her to go and stay with them and Beth and the tribe would join them for a family day. If Alex was to be alone, perhaps she should invite him to join them.

On the other hand, it would start her mother planning weddings and organising bridesmaids. It was for that reason she had never shared any male friends she had with the family. Beth was nearly as bad, telling her at every opportunity that it was about time she was settled and having more grandchildren for her parents to spoil.

"I don't know what you plan on doing for Christmas?" Alex said when they were out riding together one Saturday.

"Family of course. There's a three line whip out for a family Christmas. I daren't even think of anything else. What about you?"

"Mother. She's insisting on coming down

to stay with me. Needs to see what I'm doing with the place. I've abandoned work in the lounge and they're doing a bedroom for her. I'm dreading it and was going to ask if you'd come over at some point and help me entertain her. I'm only taking the actual bank holidays off work so she won't be here for too long."

Sarah felt a mixture of emotions. He was inviting her to meet what family he had. That must be a significant development in their relationship.

"I thought you might be going to visit her. Does she drive or do you have to collect her?"

"She drives. She's quite an independent lady really. I just dread having to cope with her on my own."

"Perhaps Mrs Harper will come and cook for you."

"Maddy? No, she'll be going to some friends."

"I wondered what her name was. You always sound so formal with her, calling her Mrs Harper."

They rode back to the Manor and groomed the horses. The two pups, now named Phoebe and Sophie were growing fast. Apart from occasional accidents, they had been house trained very quickly, largely thanks to the efforts of the estimable Mrs Harper, whose patience seemed endless.

They were out in the little yard outside the utility room and yapping for attention when the two riders had returned. Sarah took them out to the lawn and hurled balls for them to chase. She heard Alex calling her for lunch and gathered the dog toys together, calling to them to follow her.

"Soup and homemade bread today," he announced. "Shall we have a bar snack this evening? Then there's a concert on television I'd quite like to watch."

She was surprised to find it was a major rock group he wanted to watch, She had expected a classical concert or an opera and was delighted, as it was one of her own favourite bands.

"We don't know all that much about each other, do we? I think I know you and then you completely surprise me with something like that."

"Takes a long time to truly know someone. But I do think we're getting there. Don't you?"

She frowned slightly. Their relationship had been totally platonic so far. Apart from the occasional peck on the cheek when they were greeting or leaving each other, they hadn't ever kissed properly.

"I suppose. But I always think you're something of an enigma. Two quite different people. At work, I seem to be right out of your orbit but outside, you are easy going, friendly and fun to be with."

"It's all an act. I daren't let go at work. I have a difficult enough time of it with much older partners who think I'm invading their territory. Or territory they think should be theirs. But they are so out of touch.

"Dear Ken has let everyone do their own thing for so long that the practice is in serious danger of going under. I have to pull it round for all our sakes." He paused and looked upset. "Now look what's happened. We've broken a cardinal rule. We don't talk about work outside the office. Who knows what I might let slip?"

Christmas came and went in the usual flurry of preparations, over-eating and the loving family Sarah had always known. She fended off all questions about a man in her life and managed to avoid answering about who was looking after Major during her absence. She made her escape the morning after Boxing Day, using Major as her excuse. Besides, she was missing both Major and Alex and wanted to see them both. She called his mobile as soon as she was home.

"Is it all right for me to drive over and see Major this afternoon?" she asked.

"Better if you don't mind leaving it till tomorrow. I'm at work and have left my mother at home. She's leaving first thing tomorrow and would only interrogate you to find out every minute detail about you, your family and what might be between us. What she doesn't find out, she will invent. I know my mother. I'm at the office at the moment but going home in a little while. I just called in to sort the mail and make sure everything is all right. I shall be in for a bit tomorrow but maybe we could go for a ride later?"

"Fine. I was hoping to see Major, but if you think it's best, I'll wait."

"It's been a difficult time over Christmas. I hope yours was good?"

"Not bad. The usual strings of over-indulgence. We'll speak tomorrow. Call me with a time."

"Blast," she said after they hung up. She could have stayed a bit longer with her parents. Still, she didn't want to cause any friction between Alex and his mother. Clearly things hadn't gone quite as he'd hoped. His mother sounded a bit of a dragon, she thought uncharitably.

It was almost midday before Alex called

on following day.

"Nothing wrong at the office was there?" Sarah asked.

"No, I haven't even been in. My mother lingered. She seemed quite unwilling to leave, but I finally got her to go, suggesting she needed to be home before dark. So, do you want to out this afternoon? Or as early as you like. I was force-fed an enormous breakfast so I'm not planning to eat another thing till this evening."

"I'll be over right away. After my mother's usual Christmas binge, I'm ready for an intensive diet. See you soon."

It was cold and crisp and the thin winter sun provided little warmth. It was perfect for a gallop over the beach. It was low tide and Sarah's favourite cove was deserted. It was just long enough for a good gallop over the smooth sand and they raced each other back and forth, laughing and delighted in the freedom and open space.

"Just what I needed," Alex said as they trotted back to the stable.

"Me too. And I think these horses did too. I don't suppose you went out over the holiday."

"I did go on Christmas morning. Just had to get away for an hour. I left Mother watching some service on television which seemed to please her. I'm a rotten son, I know. By the way, I've been invited for drinks with Ken and the other senior partners on New Year's day. I suppose you wouldn't like to come with me?"

"Is that a good idea? Breaks all the rules, doesn't it?"

"I guess. Oh well, another day lost to riding. I thought you might make it bearable but it would certainly set tongues wagging. Forget it. I wondered if he might have invited anyone else but evidently not. I thought this might have been his gesture in lieu of the Christmas party we didn't have."

"I assumed that was because of the infernal credit crunch. But the rest of us, well we're thinking of having a meal out one night in early January. Office staff and junior people such as myself. Just an everyone pay for themselves sort of do. I'm sure you're invited if you can bear it."

"I'd love to, if you think I won't cramp anyone's style. I'm in a difficult position really. When Ken fully retires, he wants to appoint me as head of the practice but there are some staff who won't like that.

"He'll remain on the board of course and act as consultant from time to time. But, I'm very much a hands on person. I need to be a part of the day to day workings. Oh dear, I'm doing it again. Right. From now on, all work related subjects are banned. Let's go and have a cup of tea. What are you doing for a meal this evening? Wondered if you'd like to go to the pub?"

"Why not?"

The pattern continued into the early spring. Busy times at work, where they virtually ignored each other and weekends mostly spent together, riding and sharing meals. Though Sarah was still paying her rent on the paddock and stable near her home, Major was staying at Darnley Manor. Alex refused all her offers to contribute to his keep, something she felt awkward about.

"You are giving endless advice about my re-decorating. And you've spent time shopping for furnishings with me. That's more than enough compensation," he insisted.

The lounge was almost finished and they were choosing paint and wallpaper for the beautiful entrance hall and stairs. They were torn between classical, traditional styles and the need to maximise the light.

"I really think we need to go for light coloured walls. The stairs are magnificent and the pastel colours will show them up well. You need something special to put in this space," she was saying. "A chest or an oak settle. You know the sort of thing. Like old church pews. Decorative rather than comfortable."

"Was that a car stopping outside?" Alex said suddenly. "I'm not expecting anyone." He peered out of the landing window and went pale. "Oh no. It's my mother. What on earth is she doing here? I'm sorry. I had no idea."

"That's all right. Do you want me to leave?"

"Of course not. But I'll apologise in advance."

"What?" Sarah asked incredulously. "Alex, what on earth do you mean?" But he didn't reply as he was already opening the door.

"Mother," he said. "What are you doing here?"

"Thought I'd surprise you, darling. I felt like an outing and on total impulse, I got in my car and drove down here." Her voice was slightly gruff and with clipped vowel sounds that clearly came from the more upper class, old fashioned BBC style. She could have been a character straight from Jane Austen.

Alex's accent was similar but unaffected and it certainly didn't grate in the same way. "Oh, you have someone here. Of course, an interior designer. I said you needed to get one on board."

"This is Sarah, Mother. She is actually one of my partners from the practice. She stables her horse here and is kindly helping me choose the decorations."

"How do you do, Mrs Weston." Sarah held out her hand which was ignored. The woman nodded briefly and turned back to her son.

"Oh. I thought you were getting a professional in. I'd have thought a place of this magnitude would warrant someone who knows what they are talking about."

Sarah bristled. She now knew exactly why Alex had made his advance apology. The woman was downright rude, whatever she believed her social standing to be. The Duchess, she remembered her nickname had been.

"Come and look at the lounge. It's almost finished. We just need some pieces of furniture and it will be complete." Alex was delighted with this room, for which Sarah had chosen everything.

"Oh, yes. Very nice," his mother said graciously. The pale cream walls, with a hint of warmer gold tones were complemented by a rich gold carpet. Red and gold curtains were draped round all the windows, their folds held in place by rich red ropes and tassels.

When she had suggested them, Sarah had not realised just how expensive they would be and had suggested maybe she was wrong. But he had ordered them anyway and she was delighted with the result. The red and gold theme was continued on a striped chaise longue and there were a couple more matching sofas on order.

"I expect this was all planned by a designer," Mrs Weston suggested.

"All Sarah's ideas. She's done well, hasn't she?"

"I hope you're not going to find this colour carpet stains too badly. You'll have to keep those dogs out of here. They'll ruin it. And you're a bit short of tables. A room this size needs several side tables. Stand them by the walls so you can have fresh flower arrangements. And ornaments. You have very few points of interest. I can look round some of the shops in Exeter for you. One or two good pieces will make all the difference."

"No thank you, Mother. We have definite plans for everything. I don't want to clutter the place with a mass of stuff that needs cleaning. Minimalist. Now, would you like some tea?"

"Minimalist?" she intoned. "Oh, tea? Thank you dear. Herbal if you have it."

"I can go and make it," Sarah offered. "Leave you to chat to your mother."

Alex shrugged.

"All right. Thanks. Tea bags are in the cupboard over . . ."

"I know where they are, thanks." She left the room, glad to escape for a few minutes. The arrival of Mrs Weston was a blow to their plans. They were going for a meal at one of the new local restaurants with a very good reputation.

They had booked it a couple of weeks ago as tables were much in demand and they had been wanting to try it for ages. She made the tea and looked in one of the tins to see if Mrs Harper had left any home baked goodies. There was the remains of a sponge cake, which she sliced and put on a plate. She loaded everything onto a tray and carried it through to the lounge. Alex leapt up and provided a small table for her to place the tray.

"I'll pour," he said. "Thanks for making it. You relax." He indicated a chair near his mother. He handed out tea and the sliced cake. His mother gave a sniff.

"No doilies, I see. Never mind. Do you have napkins somewhere? I thought I provided a set at Christmas."

"I'll get them," Alex said, leaving the room with a sympathetic glance at Sarah.

"Now then, tell me all about yourself. Who are your family? Are they in the County?"

"They live in Cornwall, if that's what you mean. My father is a surveyor and my mother used to teach. I have one sister who is married and has three children. I am a fully qualified solicitor and I work with Alex, as he told you."

She was prattling, she told herself. It was a nervous habit when she felt uncertain. Mrs Weston stared at her, somehow managing to look down her nose at her, making Sarah feel totally inadequate and out of place. Thankfully, Alex came back into the room.

"Sorry, Mother, but I can't find the wretched napkins. Mrs Harper has put them away somewhere. I can find you a tissue if it makes eating a piece of cake more acceptable." He could barely conceal the slight sarcasm he was feeling.

"I'll make do with a cake fork," she graciously offered. Alex left the room again in search of a fork and his mother turned on Sarah again. "I hope you don't have any aspirations about my son. He is practically betrothed to a very suitable young lady. The elder daughter of one of my oldest, dearest friends. Her father is a very important company director."

"Really," Sarah said. "I'm surprised he hasn't mentioned her. He can't have seen her for some time, as we have been working together on the house for most weekends recently. And we ride every Saturday too." She was scoring points, she knew it and probably not endearing herself to this woman. "Are you planning to stay for long?"

"I may. I needed a little break. Living alone can be tedious at times. Especially at this time of year. Since the wretched hunting ban, I haven't been able to get out and enjoy my usual pursuits."

Sarah grimaced. She did not want to engage on any debates regarding hunting. She had always hated it, despite her love of riding. She suspected that any mention of her own thoughts on the subject would cause her to be banned from the house.

At last Alex came back with some forks. Silently, he handed one to his mother and caught a glance from Sarah. She looked distressed, he realised.

"I think I should be going," Sarah said as she rose from her seat. "You must have things to talk about with your mother." Mrs

Weston gave a triumphant smile. "Good-bye, Mrs Weston. Interesting to meet you."

"Yes of course. Goodbye." The odious woman concentrated on her cake and ignored Sarah's departure.

"I'm so sorry. Was she awful to you?" Alex whispered as he took her out to her car. "What about our dinner?"

"I think you're saddled with a different dining companion. You'll have to take her instead."

"I'm so angry with her. Turning up like that. What did she say to upset you? I'll tackle her about it."

"Don't cause any more problems for yourself. I can see she's adept at inventing problems where none exist. I'm obviously totally unsuitable as a companion for you. Besides, your almost-engagement to some friend of hers is a huge barrier."

"My what?"

"Apparently, you're almost engaged to an old friend of the family. Some company director's daughter?"

"Oh, for heavens sake. She must mean Prudence Fairfax. An awful ex-hunting crony. She has a face a bit like her favourite horse and neighs rather than laughs. She neighs at almost anything anyone says, funny or not. One would need to be a total idiot to marry her."

"Alex, I had no idea you could be quite so nasty," Sarah replied, slightly shocked at his vehemence but very gratified.

"I'm sorry. My mother drives me to it. I'm sorry, my dear, Sarah. So sorry about the evening being ruined. I'll call you later." He leaned over and kissed her, full on the lips. She was even more shocked.

Gently, he helped her into her car and she drove away, her heart racing. He had just been overcome with the surprise of his mother's arrival, she told herself. She was still seething somewhat at the snobbish comments she had suffered and what was more, she had been deprived of a delicious dinner and now had to think of something to cook for herself and a lonely evening ahead.

How long would his mother be staying? Now the evenings were getting lighter, she was hoping to go and see Major after work at times. If Mrs Weston was there, that would all be spoiled. Still, she tried to console herself, Alex had promised to phone. Perhaps he would persuade his mother to leave quickly.

Her plans for Sunday were also in ruins. She hung around the house, hoping that he would ring and suggest something. But the phone remained stubbornly silent. She almost contemplated visiting her parents. It was only just over an hour away but she knew there would be questions asked. Why wasn't she out riding? What was wrong with her? Had she met someone and it wasn't working out? Why did so many parents always do that?

She knew from her other friends, particularly the unmarried ones, that they suffered in the same way when they went back home. She really loved her parents but there remained this problem.

She went for a walk and regretted the empty paddock where Major should have been. Perhaps she should bring him back. Now she could ride again, she could easily ride him back and pick up his various things later. She leaned on the gate and stared into space. A van stopped behind her. It was her old friend, Joe.

"Missing him, are you?"

"Yes, a bit. Alex has got a visitor this weekend so I'm at a loose end."

"I'm just going for a pint at the pub. Why don't you tag along? Meeting some of the old crowd. We haven't seen you around for months." He opened the door for her.

"Why not?" she agreed. "That would be great. Can we stop at the cottage so I can collect my bag and some money?"

There were a number of her old friends gathered round the bar. They welcomed her with friendly warmth and she realised she'd missed them. Most of them owned horses and they'd often gone for cross country rides, stopping off at little out of the way pubs for lunch.

These were real people, salt of the earth types, she realised. Not like the snooty Mrs Weston. Thank goodness Alex wasn't like her. It would be a nightmare working with him if he was. She simply didn't understand how people could be like that. Mind you, if he had an uncle who left him so much money, he must come from a totally different class to her.

"Penny for them?" Joe intruded on her thoughts.

"Not worth even a penny. I was just thinking how nice it is to be with all of you. I've got too involved in other things lately. We should organise one of our rides again. Anyone up for it? Next Sunday?"

Several of the group agreed and they arranged to meet the following week. She would have to get Major back to his own paddock before then, without upsetting her boss.

When she arrived at work on Monday

morning, she noticed Alex's car was already parked in its usual place. Once she had settled in her office, she buzzed his extension, hoping to speak to him. Julia, his secretary answered.

"I'm afraid Mr Weston is with a client. Can I give him a message."

"It's all right. I'll catch up with him later." It wasn't worth interrupting him, especially not on a private matter. She wondered if his mother was still staying with him or whether he'd persuaded her to go back to her own home. She doubted the latter, as he hadn't called her all day.

Hopefully, the woman to whom she had taken such an instant dislike, wouldn't stay around for too long. If Alex was at work all day, she couldn't imagine there would be anything to interest Mrs Weston. Poor Mrs Harper, she thought. She may still harbour some sort of ridiculous jealousy for that woman too but at least she seemed pleasant enough. Her emotions were still confused.

After Alex had kissed her on Saturday when she left Darnley Manor, she had believed their relationship may be moving forward. But the silence since had left her feeling uncertain of anything. She frowned. She was allowing herself to become much too involved with him. She was relying on him for her entertainment and companionship outside work. So much so that she had let her old friends disappear into the past. But that was all about to change, starting next Sunday when they planned a group ride together.

If Alex felt left out, then it was too bad. He could always join them, if he wanted to. Her phone rang, announcing her first appointment of the day. Mr Knowles. His problems were still going on.

"Come in. Do sit down. I've got some news for you. Nothing too exciting but at least we've had another contact with your ex-wife."

"That's something. Thanks. So, what does she have to say? Can I see Martha?"

"She's willing for you to take her out on Saturday afternoon, providing someone else is with you."

"Oh, for goodness sake. Back to that, is she? What does she think I'm going to do? Run away with her?"

"I suppose it's precisely that. Too many stories in the press about fathers kidnapping their own children."

"She's made sure I can't do that. I've got barely enough money to live on by the time I've paid what I'm told she needs. I can't even afford to take Martha anywhere decent if I do get to see her."

Sarah could see how upset he was and was at a loss to know what to say. It was a dreadful situation. The woman was using her own child as a blackmail tool. All too frequent these days.

It wasn't as if there had been anything wrong in his relationship with his daughter. Just that the mother has fallen out of love and seemingly, had possibly found a new partner. The court had allowed the mother custody, as often happened and poor Mr Knowles was expected to pay for the upkeep of his child in a very generous way.

"The trouble was, the level I was expected to pay was set when I had a good job. All the upset caused me to lose it and I now earn less than half of what I did. Even this job's not certain to last. I've applied for a review but the forms got lost in someone's in-tray I suppose."

"It certainly takes time. I'll see what I can do. It's a ridiculous situation." The man had been badly advised by another firm of solicitors when getting divorced and his ex-wife had managed to come away with a generous settlement and he was left paying for it.

"Thanks, but don't spend too much time on it. You explained about your fees and I simply can't pay."

"I'm certain you are now entitled to legal funding. Your change of income certainly puts you into that bracket. I'll put the process into motion. Meanwhile, at least you're going to see Martha on Saturday. Let's hope it's a nice day and then you can spend the afternoon on the beach or something." She handed him the notes she had been sent regarding the arrangements for the visit. He glanced at them and rose from his seat.

"Thanks very much, anyway. I can't wait to see my little girl again. It's been weeks. I'm so frightened she'll forget me. It would break my heart. Especially as my ex has told me it's because Martha didn't want to see me."

"Don't take any notice of that. It's something that is often said just because it's easier than having to face the truth."

Sarah showed him out to reception and went back to her office. She ticked off ten minutes on her wretched form, even though it had been almost twenty. With a sigh, she settled down to work on the various files piled on her desk.

She worked through her lunch hour, eating a sandwich Poppy had brought for her while she read various papers. She glanced at the time sheet she so hated and tried to spread out her morning's work to cover the range of clients whose files she had been reading. None of it made much sense and she felt as if she were still at school, filling in exam revision charts. This situation couldn't continue.

It was as if nobody could trust each other to do a proper day's work. She needed to talk it through with the other members of staff. See what they thought of the idea and then put it to Alex at the monthly meeting at the end of the week. All aspects of life had become much more complicated since his arrival in Cornwall.

Emotions Are In Turmoil

There had been no contact with Alex outside work. In the office, she had spoken only briefly, when he had called to ask about a client she had been dealing with. He was in no mood to chat and she felt somewhat rebuffed. It seemed a long week and she really began to think that his mother had persuaded him that she was an unsuitable companion for him.

It wasn't as if she had ever indicated that she thought of him in any way other than a companion for riding and dining together. She did admit to herself that she might possibly allow herself to fall in love with him but she was keeping a tight rein on her emotions at all times.

After all, any relationship could be as doomed as the one between Mr Knowles and his ex, whatever was thought at the time they married. She saw far too many such relationships in her work. Reality had hit Alex and his mother must have convinced him that her lack of the right social standing was causing him to waste his time on her.

Meanwhile, the difficult practice meeting was looming the next day and she had still done nothing about moving Major back to his own paddock.

The atmosphere in the boardroom was distinctly tense the next day. The senior partners were grouped at one end near to Alex, who was chairing the meeting. Sarah and the junior partners were at the other end, ready to put their points to the meeting. It seemed they all shared her views on keeping the time sheets and at least two of them said their targets were out of reach. Before anyone else had a say, Alex spoke.

"I have heard a number of complaints about the time sheets. Before you say anything, I have to tell you that we shall be keeping them for at least one more month." There was a buzz of protest round the table. Even the seniors joined in. "I know this may seem like a waste of time . . ." More sounds of disharmony, ". . . but it is a valuable exercise and it is making clear exactly how much time is spent on various tasks. This enables us to revise our pricing structure for fees."

"Does it take account of how much time we actually spend filling in the forms?" Charles whispered to Sarah. She grimaced.

"Now, on to the targets." More groans. "Some of you have failed to reach even halfway to your targets for the first month. I know the targets are related to quarterly figures but one month in, it is below what it should be in many cases."

The meeting dragged on. Several complaints were voiced but quashed. It seemed that everyone was expected to continue for another month. There was distinct unrest among most of the staff, including the seniors. Alex had a battle on his hands and if he wasn't very careful, there would be major unrest which could lead to resignations.

Ken had allowed people to work on their own for many months, if not years, and nobody liked the idea of the new broom sweeping in with all his changes. At last they were allowed to leave and return to their own offices.

"I assume we fill in time sheets for this morning as a meeting, no fees applicable," Charles said with a sardonic laugh.

"Sarah," called Alex from his place at the table. "Could you spare a moment?"

"Don't forget to note it on your sheet," Charles whispered to her. "Otherwise, you'll be accused of wasting time." She glared at him and turned back to Alex.

"Do sit here," he said indicating the chair next to him. "This isn't easy for me. I'm sorry to say but your targets are the worst of anyone's. You are way below what you should be. We need to look and see how you can improve things."

"I told you, Alex. My clients don't have the sort of money you seem to expect. I don't stand a chance of reaching your precious target."

"Then you have to try to spend less time with them. If they can't pay, they can't have an hour of your time. You have to get them in and out quickly and then deal with the problem quickly and efficiently."

"And how do you suggest I deal with the situation where I have to phone someone anything up to nine times before I can speak to the right person?"

"Get your secretary to hang on to the end of the phone and let her put through the call when they have reached the right person."

"Oh yes, and which secretary would that be? I share Poppy and Chloe with at least four other people. They simply don't have time for it. I don't have my own personal Julia to do all these tasks for me." She felt herself going red with anger. He was allowing their personal life to come into work, she was certain. His mother must have persuaded him to stop seeing her and so he was making life difficult at the office.

"Come on, Sarah. I have to get this practice back on its feet or we'll have to restructure the whole thing."

"Perhaps you'd like me to leave? Resign, as I'm clearly incompetent in your eyes?"

"Don't be ridiculous. You're good at your job and your clients are very enthusiastic about you. I've seen some of the letters from them, thanking you for your efforts."

"Then you'll surely realise I can only do the job properly if I have the time to spend on it."

Alex's mobile rang. "Excuse me. Yes, all right. Wait a moment. I'm sorry, I need to deal with this. We'll speak later."

"Don't bother. Oh I'll be over this evening to collect Major. It's time he was back in his own paddock."

"Sarah. Don't storm off like that. I'll speak to you later." But she had gone. He spoke into his mobile again. "Mother. What's wrong this time? I am at work and extremely busy."

Sarah sat at her desk fuming. She felt a mixture of anger, tempered with sadness. She felt her professional integrity was being questioned and her personal life was also taking a severe dip. The past months since Alex had entered her life, there had been so many happy times spent together.

She had enjoyed working on the Manor with him. They had spent time browsing round shops and choosing things that she had loved. The entire lounge was based almost entirely on her choices, as if it were being done for her . . . or at least that's what she might have allowed herself to dream about. They had started to make plans for some of the other rooms before Mrs Weston had come on the scene and spoilt everything. She forced herself back to her work and half-heartedly dictated a letter into her machine.

Her phone buzzed.

"Are you free, Sarah? We need to finish

our discussion." Alex sounded brusque.

"I'm not sure there is anything more to say."

"I can't leave it like this. I need to go through a few specific things with you."

"All right. Five minutes. I have a letter to finish." She dreaded another encounter and wanted a few moments to compose herself. The letter had been a fiction as she had already finished it. She was pondering over the dilemma she felt surrounding her.

Mixing business and pleasure was the mistake everyone supposed. Though they had mostly kept work and personal life totally separate, she felt certain that his obsession with her targets was as a result of his mother's influence on him. The woman wanted her out of Alex's life and the situation was making it difficult for her to work with him.

She made up her mind to seek another position but it would not be easy in this part of the world. Maybe she should transfer to another branch or maybe she should leave Cornwall altogether and make a new start. She drew in her breath to compose herself. Why should she? She loved living here. There was nowhere else she wanted to live. She walked along the corridor to Alex's office, her head held high.

"Come in," Alex called in response to her knock. She saw her last time sheet spread on his desk and felt her heart sink. Horrible thing. "I was looking through your various accounts and the clients you've seen. I have to say, you are spending much longer per client than I would have expected. And your charging rates don't always match the time you're spending with them.

"It needs tightening up. For instance, this Mr Knowles you've been working with. I see you have spent something over two hours with him during the past months, but I can't find a billing for two hours. Just one for one hour." Sarah froze, partly in anger, partly in total shock.

"You're seriously telling me you have the time to go through each client, for each member of staff and marry together hours and billing?"

"Of course not. I have an internal audit clerk who does it."

"Oh really. And what sort of salary does he or she get?"

"Enough to justify the appointment."

"And you're doing this for everyone? Not just me?"

"Eventually, yes. I picked on your account because you were so very far away from your target. I needed to see why."

"But I thought I'd explained that my workload does not merit the target you set. It isn't a matter of pushing pieces of paper around like conveyancing or probate matters. These are real people with massive problems. Traumas, even. I have to spend a bit of extra time with them simply to allow them space and time to speak openly. I have to form a relationship with them before they can truly open up.

"As for Mr Knowles, I'm trying to sort out the mess another solicitor made of his divorce settlement. Poor man was totally taken to the cleaners by his ex-wife's solicitor and badly advised by his own. He's now eligible for legal funding so I shall get that sorted immediately."

"I sympathise with all of that. But you know, we also have to minimise the number of clients with legal support. They are of course, less profitable. But the fact remains, we can't afford to carry any member of staff who isn't performing properly."

"I see. So you'd like me to resign? Or perhaps I can transfer to one of the other branches?"

"Don't be ridiculous. All I need is for you to become more realistic about what you are doing. Please, Sarah," his voice softened, "try to understand the position I'm in."

She rose from her seat and walked to the door. She did not want to hand in her resignation but was very close to it. How on earth could she have considered even liking this man, let alone thinking, of the possibility of anything more? She paused and drew in her breath, desperately trying to control what she said.

"This isn't about work, is it? It's nothing to do with my wretched targets or time sheets or anything else. It's your precious mother. Mummy, dear. She doesn't approve of me and the fact we've spent so much time together. She wants you to make a suitable match in the County Set and I'm getting in the way. Don't worry. I'll collect Major later and be out of your and her way."

She stormed out of his office, ignoring his voice calling after her. She collected her briefcase and went out to her car. "I have to leave early," she told the receptionist.

She drove away from Truro, desperate to put distance between herself and Alex. He'd be at his desk for hours longer. She hoped he was putting everyone else through the same interrogation as her but sensed he wouldn't. She drove to a quiet stretch of beach and parked.

Dressed in her business suit and high heels, walking along the sand was impossible. She kicked off her shoes, tugged down her tights and walked barefoot down the wooden steps to the beach. There were a few dogs running wildly along the beach, dashing in and out of the sea while the owners stood chatting.

She went to the edge of the sea and allowed the waves to lap over her feet. It was freezing but somehow it was also cleansing. Washing away her anger. She had probably burnt her boats with the man, she had to admit, she was beginning to care for. Was, she told herself. He was so unreasonable and didn't even listen to what she was saying. All the good intentions he had suggested when he first arrived had come to nothing. An interview room for starters? Where had that idea gone?

She wandered back up the beach to her car and drove home barefoot. The heap of wet sand that collected under the pedals would have to be cleaned out later. She usually hated a dirty car and was obsessive about keeping it tidy, but she cared about nothing in her present mood. She drove home, wishing she could go for a ride and clear her head. She made tea and sat on the back step to drink it, still barefoot and still wearing a now crumpled business suit.

Sarah cooked herself a piece of chicken

with some stir fry vegetables she had in the freezer and sat down to watch the news. An item on horses reminded her that she had suggested she would collect Major that evening. It was too late now.

She needed to organise a lift over to Darnley Manor and then to ride him back. It would be dark before she could manage it all. It would have to wait till the morning. Alex and Moonlight could have the pleasure of his company for one more night.

Perhaps Joe would be around the next day and would oblige. She knew Alex would once have insisted on being available, but under the present circumstances, she would never ask him for any sort of favour. When her phone rang, she jumped. She rushed over to it, hoping, she realised that it might be Alex with some sort of apology. Not that she expected it, of course. It was her mother.

"Hello, darling. How are you?" she asked.

"Oh, you know. End of a difficult week."

"Is everything all right, Sarah?" she asked anxiously.

"Course it is," Sarah lied. Any hint of a problem and her mother would rush down. "Don't worry, Mum. I'm just tired and it really has been a difficult week." She opened up just a little about a new boss who was very demanding.

"And how's Major?"

"He's fine. I'm meeting up with the old crowd on Sunday and we're going for a cross country hack. Lunch somewhere. You know."

"That's nice, dear. Now, Dad and I were wondering if you'd be able to come home next weekend? We really need to decide what to do for your birthday. It's a big one this year and we should celebrate properly. We thought of a party or maybe a dinner for you. What do you think?"

"Oh that's really sweet of you. But I don't want a fuss. It's bad enough being nearly thirty. I don't find it necessary to let the entire world know."

"Come home anyway, darling. I was going to suggest you drive up tomorrow but you have plans so let's make it next weekend. Beth and the kids can come over on the Sunday and we can talk through ideas. She was getting quite carried away, but I said no. You wouldn't want any of the things she was suggesting."

"All right, Mum. I'll drive up Saturday afternoon after I've had a morning ride."

"Excellent. We'll take you out for dinner in Saturday. There's a lovely new place just opened and your dad's keen to support them. Nice young couple. Bring something half decent to wear, not your usual scruffy jeans."

Sarah laughed. It was good to have a loving family around, even if they could be a pain at times. But they always meant well and wanted only the best for her.

Somehow, she needed to avoid speaking about her problems at work and the reasons behind them. She settled down again and flicked across the various channels. There was really nothing that interested her. Perhaps she should go and get a DVD from the rental shop in the village. She was in the mood for some sloppy romance, she decided. Something to let her forget her own lack of romance.

She grabbed her car keys and drove down the road. She thought she saw Alex's car pass her in the opposite direction but it was too dark to see clearly. She browsed along the racks and found something that she might enjoy, picked up a box of comfort chocolates and a bottle of wine and drove back home for her solitary evening of indulgence.

Alex's car was parked on the road outside her cottage. She was tempted to drive past but was afraid he would recognise her. Drat the man, she was thinking. She pulled into the small drive and got out of her car, clutching the carrier bag with her goodies. He strode up to her, still wearing his work clothes. He must only now be going home. One had to admire him for the hours he put in, she admitted grudgingly.

"Alex. What are you doing here?"

"Waiting for you. I saw you drive past me and hoped it was only a short journey. I was going to wait five more minutes before giving up. I did think you might be at the pub but I didn't want to intrude. I couldn't bear to leave things the way we did."

"You'd better come in. I was just getting something to watch and a bottle to share with Hugh Grant."

"Sounds wonderful. I don't suppose I could be a substitute in case he's already engaged?"

"I'm not sure it's a good idea after today. Besides, won't your mother be expecting you?"

"No. Why should she?"

"Isn't she still staying with you?"

"Course not. She left on Monday morning."

"Oh. I thought as she phoned you at work, she must still be there."

"She's been phoning me two or three times every day. Wants to know what I'm doing. Finding things wrong in her life and

127

expecting me to sort them out. I don't know what's come over her. She's always been demanding but this week, it's been ridiculous."

"Isn't it obvious? It's me. She wants to make sure you're not spending too much time with me. I'm not a suitable companion for you."

"I don't know where this is coming from, Sarah. You hinted at it at work today but I can assure you it's nothing to do with that. She certainly does not control my life."

"All the same, I'm unhappy with our situation. Mixing business and pleasure just isn't working for me. I really do have to collect Major so I can get back to my normal routine. He's too far away for me to see him every day and it's all too complicated. I'll get someone to drive me over in the morning and ride him back."

"If you really mean it, I'll come and fetch you. But surely, it isn't necessary. Besides, I think . . . no. I'll wait till tomorrow. The vet is coming to check Moonlight in the morning. I'll come over after that. Around ten-thirty if that's convenient?"

Sarah nodded. Alarm bells rang.

"All right. Thanks. The vet? Is something wrong?"

"Not really. She's been off her food for a

couple of days. Well, if you're not going to offer me a glass of that wine I see poking out of your carrier, I'd better go."

"It's only village shop plonk. Nothing you'd approve of, I'm sure." His face fell and she softened. "But you're welcome to a glass if you like."

"Thanks. It's been a pig of a week."

"You're not kidding. But, I don't want to talk about work or I'll end up yelling at you."

"OK. So what film are you watching to-night?"

"It's a slushy romance. I'm sure you'd hate it. Besides, I don't suppose you've eaten and I haven't got anything exciting in the cupboard."

"Have you got any cheese? I'd kill for a few slices of cheese on toast."

Sarah grinned. "I think I might manage that. How many slices?"

Despite their awful row, it was a companionable evening. The film was amusing as well as sloppy and he seemed to enjoy it, even if he did fall asleep during the middle of it. He got up to leave soon after ten o'clock. He looked as if he was about to say something but changed his mind and gave her cheek a friendly peck.

"See you in the morning."

"Fine. Thanks." She watched as he drove away. She went inside and poured out the last glass of wine. She sat staring at her television, contemplating the day and the evening. How could Alex be two such different people?

She could hardly believe they had just spent a companionable evening together, when just a few hours earlier she was planning to change her job because he was so unreasonable. And she had decided to hate him for ever. All the same, Major still needed to come home.

She was ready and waiting at ten-thirty the next morning. She had dressed in her riding gear so she could ride straight back. There was no point in prolonging things by chatting and having lunch, as they had been used to doing over the past weeks. Was it really only last week that life looked promising with Alex around?

She thought about their conversation last night. He had never properly denied that she was right about his mother and her influence. Apart from his rudeness about Prudence whatever her name was, he'd made no mention of anything. He hadn't even apologised for failing to call her last weekend, as he'd promised, especially after that kiss. She glanced at her watch. Ten forty-five. It was most unlike Alex to be late. Perhaps the vet had been late arriving. She was on the verge of calling him at eleven o'clock when she saw his car turning into her drive.

"Sorry. The vet was late." He looked excited about something.

"I guessed as much. I hope there's nothing wrong?"

"No. It's fine. I'll tell you when we get there."

She stared at him as they made the short journey. But he said nothing. What on earth was wrong with him? He pulled up outside the back door.

"Come in."

"I was planning to ride straight back."

"Later. There's some news." He opened the fridge and took out a bottle of champagne. "Something to celebrate." Sarah could not think what was coming and accepted the glass he held out. Was he engaged or something? "You can't take Major away. You see, Moonlight is in foal. Isn't that terrific? Major is going to be a father. I knew they were keen on each other but I didn't realise it's a full on affair. That's why the vet was here this morning. He confirmed it. I suspected it when she was off her food but he says there's nothing to worry about.

She's a fit and healthy expectant mother."

Sarah stared at him, scarcely believing what she was hearing. She put the glass down and without even thinking, flung herself into his arms in excitement.

"That's terrific. Wonderful news. I'm thrilled."

The two dogs bounced round barking, joining in the excitement. She realised what she was doing and pulled away from Alex. But his arms held her tightly. "I'm sorry," she said pushing him away again. "I got carried away for a moment."

"Don't push me away. Sarah. Dear Sarah, I'm sorry I had to be so awful to you at work yesterday. The trouble is, I think I might be falling in love with you and it's extremely difficult to be strict with you at work, but I have to do it. I must come over as a dreadful tyrant."

This time, she did extricate herself from his arms. She scarcely heard anything else he was saying. He'd said he was falling in love with her. Was it really true? Was it what she wanted? His usually cool grey eyes looked slightly misty, a softer colour all together. "Say something to me."

"I'm at a loss. I am fond of you but there is too much baggage between us. We've proved that working together is far from easy. And there's your mother. She doesn't approve of me." She simply dared not admit she had, at times, been having similar thoughts to his.

"Forget about her. She'll never approve of anyone I choose, unless she thinks she made the choice first. She's a control freak as well as a snob. I will never allow her to dictate to me what I do with my life. But, we'll have to keep quiet about things at work. It wouldn't do either of us any favours."

"It wouldn't happen. Look at the gossip that ensued when you were giving me lifts into work. They were all madly speculating about us. Then when Major came to be stabled here, it all started over again. I'm sorry Alex. Much as I'd like us to be more than friends, it can't happen. Not while you're my boss and I'm just a junior partner."

A stricken look came into his eyes and his jaw tightened. The happy smile that had been lighting up his face had left it. She felt terrible. It was as if she had snatched a favourite toy from a small child. "But, let's celebrate Moonlight's news," she suggested, lifting the champagne glass again. Half heartedly, he raised his own glass, all his joy of the occasion now departed.

"It means I won't be able to ride her for

much longer," he said flatly. "I'd thought of getting another horse, maybe on loan for a few months. So, shall we have a bit of a ride this morning?" He tried to force a smile on to his face.

"I don't know what to say now. I really want Major back at home. I shall soon be able to ride in the evenings now it's getting dark so much later. And I'm going for a cross country ride tomorrow with some old friends. We're meeting in my village so I don't want to give Major too far to go in one ride."

"If you insist. But we'll ride back with you. I doubt that will be too much for Moonlight at this stage. But she's going to be very distressed to be on her own again. Especially in her present state."

"Lets see how it goes."

Major was pleased to see his old, familiar paddock and when he was unsaddled, he galloped round, familiarising himself with his old haunts. Alex and Moonlight left them and she could hear the mare whinnying as she left her companion behind. Major went over to the fence and whinnied in response. Sarah petted him and whispered her apologies to him.

"Sorry boy," she said softly. 'But you'll

soon be used to be being back here again. I'll see you each morning again and we'll go for some rides in the evenings." But she could have sworn the horse had an anxious look in his eyes. He was watching the road to see if his friend was coming back.

Most of the rest of the day was spent doing her chores. She did her washing and cleaned the cottage. Whatever she was doing, she couldn't get the thought of what Alex had said out of her mind. He was falling in love with her.

He and his family were out of her reach.

It was a pleasant outing the next day with her old friends. "Such a beautiful time of year," Sarah said dreamily.

"So what's happening with the new owner of Darnley?" asked one of the girls. "We heard he was stabling your horse."

"Nothing really. We work together. He offered to stable Major while my arm was broken. He's back home in his own paddock now."

"But you've been seeing much more of him than just at your office. One of the workers up there said you were always around choosing paint and stuff. What's going on?"

"Nothing. I was helping him modernise

the place."

"Pardon me if I don't believe you. You've been building a nest for yourself. How about letting me rent your cottage when you move into the Manor? I could never afford to buy anything around here."

"You'd better keep looking, Angela. I'm definitely not moving into Darnley Manor. Alex Weston and I have no plans. None at all."

If she said it often enough, she might one day believe it.

"Am I Your Official Escort?"

Life at Milligan, Jones and Partners had become extremely difficult for Sarah. She tried her utmost to improve her time-keeping and client billing, if only so that she was not faced with another horrid interview with Alex. He had also been avoiding her all week.

If either of them had met in the corridor, they nodded politely and stepped aside. It was tense and unpleasant. Sarah was relieved to be going to see her parents by the time the weekend arrived. Poppy saw her as she was leaving on Friday evening.

"So, there's trouble in paradise I gather,"

she suggested cheekily.

"Don't know what you mean," came Sarah's cool reply.

"Come on. You and Prince Not-So-Charming have been going round avoiding each other and looking grim the whole week."

"Prince Not-So-Charming?"

"Alex. Our potential new lord and master. He's even sounded off at the highly esteemed Julia on a couple of occasions. Something or someone is rattling his cage. The office grapevine insists that there's some rift between their favourite family law specialist and him."

"Then the office grapevine is wrong on all counts. There was never anything between us for a rift to have developed. He merely helped me out when my arm was broken and kindly stabled my horse."

"And all the shopping expeditions together? Looking round antique shops. Choosing paint. Nothing gets past us, you know."

"Then it's time you found something better to do with your lives. Have a good weekend. I'm going home to see my parents. On my own." She swung out of the office and got angrily into her car. If Alex ever heard any of that, he would understand precisely why it could never work between them.

She went home to change and then across to see Major. She took a couple of apples for him and called him over. He was standing at the corner of his field, staring down the lane where he had last seen Moonlight departing. She called him. He turned his head but resumed his gaze down the lane.

"Hey boy, what is it?" Sarah asked as she crossed over to him. "Are you missing your lady friend?" She held out the apple, usually his favourite treat. He nibbled at it, almost as a gesture of 'thanks, but no thanks' and let the rest of it fall to the ground. "Oh dear, you have got it bad haven't you?"

She looked at the sky. Stormy clouds were gathering over the distant sea. "I think I'd better put you inside the stable before the rain comes. It's still cold at night, isn't it?" She slipped his head collar on and led him inside. He was not a happy horse at all.

She continued to chat to him and he nuzzled her, as if asking why everything had changed again. "I'm sorry, but it was only ever a temporary arrangement. One day we shall see Moonlight again." He lifted his head as if he understood and gave a small whinny.

She patted him and feeling even more troubled, shut the door and went back home. Why had Alex come into her life and caused all this upset? She was even finding her time spent at home rather lonely. Before he had arrived, she had been quite content to entertain herself and rarely ever felt bored. She'd been happy to go to the local pub for supper occasionally, knowing she would meet friends there for companionship. Snap out of it, she ordered herself.

She changed out of her horse clothes and put on clean jeans and shirt and set off down the road to the village. She had nothing special planned for supper so she would eat out and hope to meet someone to talk to. She needed cheering up.

The pub was virtually empty when she arrived. So much for finding someone to talk to.

"Where is everyone?" she asked. "You're usually busy on a Friday night."

"They've got a quiz night on in the next village. Bit of a competition going on between the two of us. They were all here last week. Packed out we were. Now, what can I get you? We've got some lovely freshly home-made pies."

"Sounds good to me. I might have a beer to go with it for a change."

139

"Make that two," said a voice from the doorway. Sarah swung round.

"What on earth are you doing here, Alex?"

"I saw the lights were off at the cottage. I saw the car still parked outside so guessed you must have walked somewhere and wondered if you were here."

"Quite the detective, aren't you?"

"Do you mind if I join you?"

"I'm not really sure. Depends what you want to talk about."

"Anything. Nothing. Horses. How's Major?"

"I'm a bit worried about him. He seems to be fretting."

"Missing Moonlight do you think? I must say, she's not herself. I think she's missing him. What should we do about it?"

"I don't know. It certainly isn't a good idea for us to live in each other's pockets as we have been doing. Did you know that they're even talking about us around here? I had such a job on Sunday to dispel the rumours. Evidently we've been seen shopping together and speculation is running rife. I was even asked if I'd let my cottage to one of them when I move in with you. However much you want to be discreet, it's hopeless in an area with such a closed shop attitude."

"So, either we see nothing of each other

and let our horses both die of broken hearts or bite the bullet and you and I seriously become an item, as they say these days."

"I'm flattered Alex, truly I am. But I know I'm not ready to settle down, especially not with someone I have to work with. I'm sorry, but this has to be the last time we share a meal. When you've seen as many divorce cases and family break-downs as I have, you'd understand why I'm too scared to get any closer.

"As for the horses, they'll get over it once they settle back into their routine. It's ridiculous to suggest they might die if they don't see each other. Horses don't have broken hearts."

They were spared further conversation as the meal arrived.

"That looks marvellous, thank you," Alex remarked to the waitress. "I'm starving. Didn't get round to lunch today. Not even a sandwich."

"And you haven't been home yet either."

"How do you know that? Oh, the business suit, I suppose." She nodded. "This is wonderful food. Shame if it really is the last time we shall share a meal."

"Alex," Sarah said with a warning note. "I'm sorry. I'm sure you're a lovely man. Some of the time," she added. "But we can't fall in love. Believe me. We simply can't. Just because we share a love of horses doesn't mean we can share anything more."

"There's rock music too. We both like that. And I love what you've done to my house. And I did watch a soppy film with you." It was hard to believe this was the same man who had given her such a hard time at work.

"All right. We do have some things in common. But you're embarrassing me. I'll never see eye to eye with you about work." She held up her hand. "No, I'm not going to talk about work, but that proves there's a huge gulf between us. I care too much about people to be sufficiently businesslike for you and I see it as a great divide we will never get over."

He gave a shrug. "I won't mention it again. I trust you'll allow me to pay for the meal?"

"Well, thanks. If you like. I'm happy to go halves."

He rose and went to pay the landlord. She got up and pulled on her jacket. "Thank you," she said as he came back to the table.

"Can I drop you back home?"

"I don't mind walking." They went outside and saw it was pouring with rain. "Actually, I'll change my mind. I came out without a coat. A lift would be great."

"Thought you might. Any plans for the weekend?"

"I hope to ride in the morning and then I'm going to see my parents. My sister and family are coming over on Sunday."

"Sounds nice," he said almost wistfully. "I think I'll get some work done. And I need to make a start on organising the bedrooms. They've nearly finished the major building work. The heating's all done round the house too. Lovely and warm now and the damp is disappearing fast. Right. Here we are. Have a nice weekend."

"You too. Thanks for supper and the lift."

"Night, Sarah."

He drove away, his heart sad with failure. He cursed himself for rushing her. He was such a loser where women were concerned. He wasn't that bad looking. But still he failed to attract the woman he truly wanted. If anything, it was worse since he had inherited his uncle's fortune. His mother had convinced him that every woman who showed an interest in him was simply after his money.

Not very flattering for a mother to think that, he thought, but perhaps she was right. He had to face it, at almost thirty-five, he needed to settle down. He had put so much time and effort into his career and now into making Darnley Manor a beautiful place to live, he hadn't even thought of meeting anyone other than Sarah.

Perhaps that was the problem. He was falling in love with her because she really was the only person he had met recently. Apart from Maddy Harper. But goodness, the most she ever talked about was the animals and what he'd like for supper. Hardly marriage material.

"At least you two give me a warm welcome," he said to his pups as he let them out. "All wagging tails and happiness, aren't you? Come on then. Let's go and see if Moonlight's safely tucked in."

Sarah spent a restless night tossing and turning. The sad look on Alex's face haunted her. He was certainly a catch, she told herself. What was holding her back? She forced herself to think about his uncompromising attitude to her work. Anyone who could be so uncompromising was not for her.

It was much too wet to go riding the next morning. She let Major out into the paddock for a good run and then shut him in his stable in the early afternoon. She left him plenty of fresh hay and filled the large trough with water. She would be back in plenty of time the next day, to feed him and muck out the stable.

If the weather was more reliable, she'd risk leaving him out but, in his present mood he'd probably stand out in the rain, gazing lovelorn down the lane and then catch a chill from being soaked through.

"Bye Major. See you tomorrow." She patted him and left the top of the door open just a little way.

Her parents greeted her as warmly as ever. Her mother stood back and looked at her after her first hug.

"You're looking pale. Doesn't she look pale, Jack?" Her father nodded, winking at Sarah as he did so. It was a standing joke. Her mother always needed Jack to confirm that she was right about whatever it was concerning their children.

"You always say that. I've had a busy week and I'm just a bit tired. Looking forward to being spoiled this weekend. Are Beth and the tribe coming over tomorrow?"

"They'll be here for lunch at twelve. I expect you'll want to get back to that horse of yours before it gets dark."

"Yes, of course. I've had to leave him in the stable. It was so wet when I left. I didn't want him to stand out and get a chill."

"How's work really been?" her mother asked. "You said it was hectic. Why's that, especially? What happened to the chap who was stabling the horse?"

"Leave the poor girl alone," her father intervened. "Questions, questions. It's like the Spanish inquisition when you get going."

"I'm just interested to know what's going on in our daughter's life."

"Why don't you make us some tea? And I know you made one of your chocolate cakes. Let's have a slice to go with the cuppa."

"That's for tomorrow. We don't want to spoil our dinner tonight, do we?"

The banter went on between her parents and she sat back, listening with some pleasure. Nothing had changed in all their lives and she found it very comforting. Her mother went to make tea and she spoke to her father.

"Does Mum chat away like this when there's just the two of you?"

"Usually."

"So, how do you cope?"

"I've learned to say yes and no in the right order. I occasionally get it wrong and she realises I was never actually listening. But you know, it's a part of your mother and our relationship. I love her dearly, of course but I can't listen to everything she says."

"How did you know she was the right one?"

"I just did. She was the only one for me from the moment we met."

"And you for her, I suppose?"

"Well no. She was involved with some engineer from somewhere near Exeter. I had to be patient for quite a few months until I won the battle. Sheer persistence and dogged determination."

Sarah stared at him. It was difficult to imagine her father as a young determined man, chasing her mother. He smiled and indicated her to keep quiet as her mother came back into the room.

"I relented and cut you a slice of chocolate cake. By the time they've eaten a large Sunday lunch, they won't all demand big slices of cake. It won't spoil your meal, will it?"

"Course not. I'm starving. It's so good to be home," Sarah said as she bit off a large mouthful of her mother's most special of all comfort foods. Alex could get lost.

After a large meal and with her mind taken off her worries, Sarah slept peacefully. Her mother woke her at ten o'clock the next morning.

"I can't believe I slept so late. You should have woken me."

"There's a coffee for you. And I've brought you some breakfast. Just toast and cereal as it's late."

"Wonderful. You're spoiling me and I'm loving it."

"You should come up more often. I keep saying to your father, we don't see nearly enough of you. Now eat up before it gets too cold."

The subject of her impending birthday had not been mentioned the previous day. They must be waiting for Beth to make the attack. It was pointless resisting their plans. If she did, they would only plan some dreadful surprise party and she would be expected to be surprised. If she agreed to something, at least she might have a little say in the matter.

When Beth and Mike arrived with their three children, the house was filled with noise and laughter. Beth was similar in looks to her sister, another blue-eyed blonde, but much more rounded after her years as a mum and housewife. The sisters had always been good friends, though Beth had been serious about Mike for so long it was hard to remember life without him around.

He was an accountant, a family man who

adored his wife and children. The three little boys were being beautifully brought up and were polite, though extremely noisy at times. Mrs Pennyweather was delighted to have all her brood around and busied herself with vegetables and basting meat while she chatted to her two daughters. Her husband arrived with glasses of sherry in the true family tradition and they all toasted each other, as they had done for most of the girls' adult lives.

"So, has Mum explained the plans for your thirtieth?" Beth asked.

"Of course not, dear. I was leaving it all to you," her mother replied.

"Right. Well, it's on a Sunday so we thought a party on Saturday night for the friends and family and lunch at one of the hotels on Sunday. Lunch just for close family of course."

"That sounds like an awful lot of fuss. Please though, make sure people don't buy me presents. I really don't want people spending money they can't afford and I don't want the embarrassment of a mound of presents. Anyway, can't we just do the lunch? Then it isn't so much work for Mum."

"Certainly not. Besides, there're loads of people who want to come to the party.

Several old school friends and one or two from university days."

"It sounds as though you've already got it planned."

"Well yes. We needed to make a start early to make sure people would get here." Beth was in full swing now. "And as you're still showing no signs of settling down we decided we needed to invite plenty of single men. It's high time we got you sorted out."

"How dare you?" Sarah protested. "I simply . . ."

"Oh shut up, sister mine. I want some nieces and nephews before I'm drawing my pension."

"I'm a career girl. I have no intention of producing any nieces and nephews or grandchildren of any sort. If I want a partner, I can provide my own, thank you very much."

"I knew it," her mother said triumphantly. "It's this man who was stabling your horse. You've been seeing him, haven't you?"

Sarah's heart sank. What a dilemma. If she said she had been seeing him, her mother would be making plans. If she denied it, they would pair her off with some boring male she would hate.

"All right, yes. We work together and I have been seeing him occasionally. I've been helping him choose paint and colour schemes for his new house. He lives fairly close and it was helpful to keep Major at his place when I had my broken arm. But that's all it is."

"But you'll invite him to the party, won't you? And he can have Beth's old room to stay over for the lunch the next day. Oh, this is all going to be such fun." Sarah closed her eyes as her mother prattled on, making her plans. It was simply easier to give in, than to protest, though what Alex would make of it all, she dreaded to think. She needed to explain it all to him before the invitation arrived. She just hoped he had a prior engagement and wouldn't be free to come.

Lunch was her mother's usual wonderful standard. Roast beef, light, crispy Yorkshire puddings and fresh vegetables aplenty. Apple pie and clotted cream followed.

"That was enough of a cholesterol fix to last me for weeks," said her father. "It'll be back on the bran flakes for the rest of the week."

"They need feeding up occasionally," Mrs Pennyweather said with a beam. "Oh, I can't tell you how lovely it is to have you all here. And it's only two more weeks before the whole family from everywhere around will be here too."

As Sarah drove home some time later, she contemplated the plans that had been whirled past her, giving her no chance to protest, disagree or even add her own requests. She smiled and accepted that it might be fun, if only Alex was too busy to join them.

Somehow, she needed to convince him that this was not an acceptance of some sort of relationship. At least she had persuaded everyone to leave the invitation to her and so didn't have to give them his address as Darnley Manor. If they thought he owned a manor house, they would be even more excited.

It was all getting much too complicated. She would leave inviting him for another week and then he would be less likely to be free. She could fend off questions from her sister or mother for a while longer, if necessary.

She stopped at the cottage to change and went straight over to see Major. He was standing with his head hanging over the stable door and he seemed pleased to see her. She let him out and he galloped across the paddock, inevitably ending up at the corner to stare down the lane again.

He had eaten virtually none of the food

she had left out. It was very worrying and she wondered if she might need to consult the vet. Maybe if Moonlight wasn't going to be ridden in a few months, she might come and stay with Major in his paddock. In the summer, they didn't need to be stabled overnight so it might work. But then, they would have to be parted again once Moonlight was ready to have her foal. It was worse than having a lovesick teenager around.

All the same, she was concerned about her beloved horse. She cleared out the stable and put down fresh straw. She filled his hay net and hung it on the hook. Finally, she washed out the trough and re-filled it with fresh water. She called to Major to come and he trotted across the paddock and she fed him some of his favourite dry food.

"You take as much looking after as a lovesick teenager too, don't you?" This time, she left the stable door open so he could shelter if he wanted to. It was much warmer today and there was no sign of rain.

Back at her cottage, she made some tea and sat down feeling exhausted and still very full. No supper for her that evening, after her mother's feeding frenzy. She reflected on the weekend and the plans that were being made to celebrate her birthday.

She could always forget to invite Alex. He

need know nothing about any of it and she could let her mother know nearer the time that he wouldn't be coming. This was certainly the best plan she could come up with. There was no way they could send him an invitation to work as they had no idea of his name. She had made sure of that.

Meanwhile, she had another difficult week to face. Seeing Alex every day, knowing that he thought he cared for her was always going to be a problem. She was also afraid that if she allowed herself to, she might easily fall in love with him. It was becoming a totally impossible situation. Perhaps she really did need to find another practice.

It was a busy week, with a couple of days spent in court and very little chance of seeing Alex at all. Though she missed him and his companionship for riding at the weekend, she went out with her group of friends for a Sunday ride. There had been numerous phone calls from her sister and mother regarding the party, but she had managed to put them all off, especially about Alex's invitation.

"I'm sure he'll be there," she said several times over on each call. She kept her fingers crossed as she spoke, just in case it was bad luck to fib.

All was well until the Wednesday before

her birthday. She was chatting to Poppy in reception when the secretary suddenly remembered.

"Hey, it's your birthday this weekend. Are we going to celebrate in style? After all, it is a biggy, isn't it? A significant move towards middle age."

"Thanks a bunch. I don't need to be reminded."

"Well, what are we going to do about it? Drinks after work on Friday at the very least."

"All right. But my mother and sister have a party planned at their place for Saturday. It'll be mostly people and old friends from up there so I haven't asked any of the office people. It would be a nice idea to have drinks after work. Wine bar, do you think? Or shall I get some nibbles in and we can have it here?"

"Leave it all to us. Here I think. Then we can be silly without the world knowing. I'll clear it with the powers that be." Poppy was already pulling a pad over to begin making lists.

"Fine. Many thanks. Just make it clear, I don't want any presents. I really mean it. No collections for the aging Sarah. It's bad enough having parents trying to match me up with some ghastly male so I can produce lots more grandchildren for them."

"What's all this?" Alex asked as he came into the reception. "Who's having grandchildren?"

"Nobody."

"Then who is trying to find a partner for you?"

"Alex, please," Sarah protested, blushing furiously.

"Her parents have organised a party to celebrate her birthday and they are trying to find her a man. They think it's time she settled down. It is her thirtieth birthday after all." Poppy had a wicked grin on her face.

"Well thanks for all that," Sarah said with heavy sarcasm. Alex now knew everything she had been trying to keep secret for the past week.

"If it's all right with you," Poppy was continuing, "we'd like to have a few drinks in the office on Friday after work. Celebrate the occasion. Just some wine and a few nibbles. Everyone welcome."

"Sounds like an excellent idea. Count me in. Are we all chipping in?"

"Unless the firm want to pay, of course," Poppy asked hopefully.

"Leave it with me. We can at least contribute, even if not pay, for the whole thing.

Creating precedents and so on."

"How like a lawyer," Poppy replied. "But thanks anyway."

"No worries. Actually Sarah, I need a word, if you're free."

She closed her eyes as if in supplication and then followed him to his office.

"I know this isn't the right moment, but I've scarcely seen you for the past couple of weeks. I'm really worried about Moonlight. I'm wondering if you would consider letting Major come back to us? Even if only for a while. My mare is off her food. She's listless and unenthusiastic about everything and the vet says there's nothing physically wrong. But being pregnant, she does need to keep up her strength."

"I must say, I was wondering if Moonlight might come and stay with us. Major is also pining. I told him he was like a lovelorn teenager. Let me think about it for a while. Actually, it might solve a bit of a problem. I'm going to my parents for the weekend and I haven't got anyone to look after him. I was going to leave him just overnight and get back as early as I can. It wouldn't go down well as they have massive plans for parties and lunches."

"Sounds wonderful," he said sadly. "I hope you enjoy it." He looked so miserable, she suddenly felt sorry for him. Against all her better judgement, she invited him to accompany her.

"Are you sure?"

"Well, yes," she said, immediately regretting it.

"Then I'd love to come. Am I your official escort or just someone from the office? Is it formal or casual?"

"You'd sort of be my official escort, if that's all right with you. Don't get carried away. It doesn't mean anything. You'd really be there to stop my mother attempting to marry me off to the first single male she can lay her hands on.

"They said you can stay over in my sister's old room and have lunch . . . on . . . the Sunday." She slowed right down, realising she had let out the fact that he was already expected.

"I see. So when exactly were going to ask me?"

She pulled a face.

"Sorry, but I wasn't really going to say anything. I was going to tell them you had other plans. Sorry. It's just that things have been difficult between us."

His face twitched into a grin.

"It's fine. I totally understand. But I shall be delighted to accompany you in whatever

158

capacity. Shall we drive up together? And what about these two teenagers of ours? Shall we let them get back together?"

"I could ride Major over this evening, if you like. But please, don't try to push me into anything more."

"I shall be the soul of discretion. I won't even suggest you stay for supper. I can easily feed any spare food to the dogs."

"How are they? Bet they've grown."

"They're fine. Great fun and your suggestion of having two has worked very well. They are a mini pack and do everything together. We'll finalise details for the weekend when I see you this evening. Sure you're OK to ride over? I can easily fetch him in the trailer."

"No. I'll enjoy a ride and it's plenty light enough."

"Thanks, Sarah. I shall look forward to cessation of hostilities. I've missed you."

Alex Makes An Impression

Once he realised where they were going, Major had to be held back from a gallop. He was tossing his head and clearly excited. They trotted past the paddock where he and Moonlight had spent so much time and began to neigh.

Moonlight replied to him from the stable yard as Sarah rode in. Alex was waiting and opened the gate for her. It was a delight to watch the two horses' greetings as they nuzzled each other and showed obvious pleasure at being together again.

"Looks like we made the right choice. Do you want to rub him down and put him inside?" Alex led his horse into her stable and Sarah took Major into his loose box in the same building, so they were very close to each other. When she had him settled, Alex invited her to look round the house to see the latest progress.

The two puppies saw her and greeted her like a long lost friend. They were running round her, yapping and with tails wagging like windmills.

"Hello, you two. Haven't you grown?" She fussed them, rubbing their tummies as they rolled over, each demanding her attention. They bounced up again, barking in their excitement.

"Go out now, you horrible pair," Alex said with great affection. "We can't hear ourselves think." He pushed them into the yard and left them to get rid of some of their boundless energy. He led the way into the dining room. "I think you were right about the colour. This slightly paler version of the

Wedgewood blue had kept it looking light. And what do you think of the cornices? I like the white against the blue. Reminds me of Wedgewood china."

"It's beautiful. The whole thing looks wonderful. Bit short on furniture mind you. Unless you plan to dine Japanese style, lying down on the floor on cushions." She examined everything carefully. "And those curtains are perfect." Blue and white brocade gave the right air of formality to the room but kept it light. It was a north facing room so suffered a little from having poorer quality daylight filtering in through the trees. "Are you planning to cut down some of the trees?" she asked.

"I decided not to. As this room will only be used at night, the lack of light doesn't matter too much. I just need a dining suite now. Big table and a set of chairs." He looked at her hopefully but she said nothing.

"Now, do you want something to eat or shall I drive you home right away?"

She frowned. She could already smell a delicious savoury smell coming from the oven. Despite all they had said, it was just too tempting.

"How can I resist? Thank you. But . . ."

"I know. I mustn't think you are changing

your mind. Actually you know, I decided I can't be bothered about office gossip any more. Those girls will gossip whether there is anything or nothing. Now, let's eat. Tell me more about this weekend. Exactly how do you want me to play it? Casual friend? Ardent admirer?"

She stared at him. He seemed like a different man to the one she had been getting to know recently. He was funny, light-hearted and seemed genuinely pleased to be involved in the coming events. Could she have misjudged him?

"Just a friend, please," Sarah suggested.

"A good one though. I'll promise to behave myself. No mention of work, of course. So what do you think? Shall we drive there together?"

"I think maybe separate cars. Then you can escape if you want to without having to wait for me. You might find my family a bit much to cope with. I expect they will have invited a mass of people and you won't know any of them. I shall quite understand if you want to duck out after the party and not wait for the lunch next day. Honestly, why they have to go so over the top, I just don't know."

"They sound like the sort of family most people would dream of. Close and loving.

Don't knock it. You could have a dragon of a mother like mine."

"Alex, what a thing to say."

"Unkind, but don't forget I've lived with her all my life. She's a very demanding woman and very manipulative. You've no idea of some of the things she's done to make sure I'm available for her whenever she thinks she needs me."

Sarah was more than a little shocked to hear what he had to say. She had often accused her own mother of trying to organise her life for her but it was nothing like Alex was describing. She had the feeling that his mother asked him to do what was best for her whereas her own mother always did what was best for her daughter.

All the teasing about not settling down did hold a grain of truth, but it was more in fun than anything too serious. Both parents and even Beth, though she would never have admitted it, were proud of what she had accomplished.

Once the meal was over, Alex drove Sarah back to her cottage. It was late and she felt quite exhausted. An early night was called for, she decided. She lay in bed, wondering if she'd done the right thing in inviting Alex to the party. She must not get too involved with him. She liked the way they shared so many things and wanted that to continue.

She dreamt about him and in her dreams, things were much more serious than in real life. She even dreamt they were married and felt oddly confused when she awoke, trying to remember the wedding. She sat up in bed and shook her head, trying to reconcile reality with her fantasy world. Her alarm told it was only five-thirty.

Much too early to get up. She lay back down and thought she might go and see Major, until she remembered he wasn't in his own stable. At six o'clock she got up anyway and took a leisurely shower. She needed to find something to wear at the weekend and spent half-an-hour trying things on until she had made a shortlist.

She left a couple of outfits on the bed so she could choose between them later. Maybe she should have bought something new. If she had time at lunch, she would make a trip out to the shops and see if she could find something. Now that Alex was accompanying her, she decided she needed to make a bit more of an effort.

Poppy was full of plans when she met her later in the day.

"Alex has authorised some money we can

spend on nibbles and things. We all decided that it might be an idea to get a takeaway sent in for later so we can all enjoy a meal as well and we don't get too tipsy to drive home again when the time comes. Some of us are driving in together as well. Can you get a lift in? A certain senior partner for instance? Now, do you want me to get you a sandwich?"

"No thanks. I'm going shopping. I need to find something gorgeous to wear for this party on Saturday. Decided my entire wardrobe is looking very tired."

"Try that little boutique place round the back of cathedral. They had some fantastic things in there. Expensive but at your level in the firm, you can afford it." Poppy gave her a wicked grin. "And who will be your partner for the evening? Anyone we know?"

"Of course not. How would anyone you know possibly be visiting my parents' home? Now, must dash or I'll never find anything." She hurried out and dashed along the narrow streets to find the boutique Poppy had suggested. She quickly looked along the rails but could see nothing that attracted her.

The trouble was, she hadn't a clue what she wanted, not even the colour or style. She left the shop and walked back towards the office. In the window of a charity shop, there was a glorious royal blue evening dress. It looked as if it was heavy silk, fairly short and with pretty beading embroidery round the top and with slim spaghetti straps. She stopped and gazed at it. A second hand dress? Could she really buy a second hand dress?

She went inside and asked the size. It was exactly her size. She asked to try it on and it was an excellent fit. Could have been made for her. It was in perfect condition and had been freshly cleaned. She knew this because the dry cleaner's tag was still attached to the exclusive designer label. Who would know she thought and so what if they did?

"I'll take it," she told the assistant.

"It's a lovely dress and just right with your colouring. For something special is it?"

"My parents are giving me a party. Thought I needed to make an effort. Who on earth would part with something like this? It's practically brand new."

"One of our regular ladies. She does a lot of entertaining and doesn't like to wear the same thing too often. We get the benefit. I'm afraid it's rather expensive but nothing like the original cost."

"Well, I was expecting I'd have to pay way over this much for something much less attractive, so I'm very happy with it. I shall come and look in here again. I'd never thought of it but when I saw it in the window, I was delighted. Thanks very much."

"Let's see," Poppy demanded when Sarah got back to the office, clutching her dress bag. "I don't recognise that bag. Where did you go in the end?"

"An exclusive little place, near the cathedral."

"Oh great. I knew they'd have something. Come on then. Show me." Sarah had taken off the dry cleaning labels as she left the shop and so was able to take out the dress without letting on where she had bought it. "Oh wow. That's fantastic. Just your colour. Makes your eyes look extra blue." She looked at the well known designer label. "Good grief. It must be some party. This must have cost you a fortune."

"Just a small one." She wondered whether to let on but decided against it. You're turning into a snob yourself, she thought. "I really need some shoes now. I'll have to look for those tomorrow or after work today, if I finish in time. Must get back now or I'll be late for my two o'clock." Feeling very pleased with herself, Sarah settled down to work, reading her notes ready for her next client.

At the end of the day, Alex stopped by her office.

"You never did tell me what I was supposed to wear for this do of yours."

"Sorry. We somehow forgot. Just a dark suit I should think. I'm not sure what Mum has got planned. Put in something casual as well. Then you'll have it covered."

"So, what are you wearing?"

"Something a bit sparkly and evening-ish. Short of course."

"Sounds good. I also need directions, address and so on. Would you like to go out this evening and discuss everything?"

"I need to get things sorted at home, but thanks anyway. I'll have to give seeing Major a miss too. Give him a pat from me and I'll come over early Saturday before I leave."

"You could always come round to see him now."

"I shall only stay on again and I do need to get some stuff done. I have a busy morning tomorrow too and need to read up on some files. Then there's the drinks thing after work. All go, isn't it?"

"I'll give you a lift in tomorrow, if you like. Then we only need one taxi home if we have a drink or two."

"I could bring you. I don't intend to have much."

"No. I insist. It isn't out of my way. You can always drive me over on Saturday to collect my car on your way to your parents. Fair deal?"

It was agreed and she left work reasonably early.

As she arrived back at her cottage, she remembered the shoes she had planned to buy. It was too bad. She needed to have a good rummage through her cupboard and see what she had stashed away.

There must be something that would do. She was turning into a regular skinflint, with her old shoes and charity shop dress. She shook it out of the bag and holding it against her, looked at herself in the long mirror in her bedroom. It was a gorgeous creation and once more, she couldn't believe how perfect it was. Charity shops were wonderful, she decided.

Sarah felt quite guilty the next day as Poppy seemed to spend much of the day organising what she had seen as her party. Chloe had good naturedly held the fort with phone calls and the typing that was urgent, to leave Poppy free to set things up.

Fortunately, the boardroom was left free

for the day and this was the obvious venue for the after-work gathering. Because of the financial constraints, there had been no staff Christmas party this year and they had all felt a bit deprived. On a smaller scale, this was some sort of compensation. There were no wives or partners invited, but most of the staff were staying on. Some of the older, more senior people were just staying for a few drinks and leaving before the food was arriving.

As Poppy said when Alex handed over an envelope containing several notes, "Don't worry about it, Alex. This is just a good excuse for a bit of relaxation and a bit of a party. It isn't setting the precedent for a celebration for everyone's birthdays."

It was a jolly evening and being the end of a busy week, everyone was rather tired and the party ended by nine o'clock. Charles had done his best to persuade Sarah to go to a club with him but she had resolutely refused, saying she was going away for the weekend and needed an early night. Alex had interrupted their conversation, asking if she was ready to leave.

"Oh, do tell me all. Is there something going on that Uncle Charles doesn't know about? Some little office affair that hasn't yet broken cover?"

"Nothing to tell. Alex is a near neighbour of mine. He gave me a lift so I didn't have to drive home. End of story."

"Something tells me that fibs are being told here. The way the two of you look at each other belies everything you say. And what's more, the lovely Sarah is always turning me down. Now if she isn't seeing someone out office hours, I need an explanation."

"Could it just be that the lovely Sarah finds you an interminable bore?" Alex said sweetly.

Charles scowled.

"If you weren't my boss in all but name, I might be compelled to challenge you to a duel."

"Perhaps you've been having too many evenings in watching Robin Hood and the like. Don't think duelling has been a part of British heritage for a good many years. Now, if you're ready, Sarah?"

"I ought to help clear up," she suggested. "You go if you want to. I can easily get a taxi."

Alex rolled up his sleeves and started collecting rubbish into a black sack. Poppy and the others stared. It was unheard of for one of the senior partners to actually do such work. Alex rose highly in their estimation.

■ ■ ■ ■

Sarah woke early on Saturday morning. She stretched and lay back, luxuriating in those few waking moments when she actually had time to enjoy them. Thirty years old. It was depressing in many ways. A new decade in one's life is always momentous, she was thinking. The inevitable approach of middle age.

She wondered how her parents must feel. It must be like having extra birthdays oneself each year, or at least another indication of the years passing, as each child had a significant birthday. She flung back her duvet and went along to her shower.

Her early rise habits were too deeply ingrained and even when she had time to be lazy, she was too impatient. She put on her old horse-riding clothes and grabbed a quick coffee. She wanted to go and see Major first thing, before she got ready for her day.

At seven o'clock, she was driving along to Darnley Manor and went into the yard, hoping she wasn't disturbing anyone. She had brought apples for both horses and went into the stable.

Major whinnied and greeted her happily.

He nuzzled her shoulder and she breathed in his scent. His chestnut coat was gleaming and smooth. Someone had been grooming him. Probably Mrs Harper, she thought. Moonlight neighed and she went over to her loose box and gave her an apple too.

"Pleased to have your handsome male back, are you? You're a very beautiful lady, aren't you."

"What a delightful picture," said a voice from the doorway. "One I could get used to. Happy birthday."

"Alex. You startled me. Thank you. Hope I didn't disturb you coming here so early."

"Not at all. I was up anyway. Have you had breakfast? I've got some croissants warming and the coffee pot's on."

"Sounds tempting, but I mustn't linger too long. I said I'd be at my parents' by ten."

"Then you've plenty of time to enjoy some breakfast. Besides, I wanted to give you your present."

"Oh Alex, you shouldn't have bought me anything."

"All right. I'll take it back to the shop. I'm sure they'll exchange it. Come and look first. You may change your mind."

They went into the warm kitchen which smelled of coffee and croissants. Sarah was glad she had taken up the invitation and noticed the table was set for two. There was a parcel, wrapped in silver foil at one place. It had an elegant bow on top and a card stood beside it. She smiled at Alex and picked it up.

"Go on, open it," he urged.

She tugged at the ribbon and gently pulled off the pretty paper. It was a box with the name of one of the best local jewellers on top. With trembling fingers she opened it. A beautiful necklace lay on the black velvet lining. It was a shower of brilliant blue stones which would exactly match her new dress.

"Oh Alex, it's perfect but it's far too much. I can't accept this," she said sadly closing the box and handing it back to him.

"They're not real stones," he assured her. "And it wasn't as expensive as it looks. And I know it will match your dress. I made Poppy tell me what you'd be wearing so this was carefully chosen. Please accept it. A gift between colleagues if you prefer to think of it that way."

"Well," she began hesitantly. "You're right about it being a perfect match for my dress. And I really love it. Thank you, but I am concerned about accepting such an expensive gift."

"Call it a thank you for all your help and

advice over the house."

She nodded gratefully and accepted his gift.

"Now, let's get some coffee inside you and some food. You've got a long day ahead."

By nine-thirty, Sarah was driving along the A30 towards her parents' home. She was going to be later than the ten o'clock she had promised but knowing her mother, saying she needed help was only a ploy to ensure her early arrival. There was more traffic than she had expected so it was a slow journey.

"You're late," her mother accused when she finally arrived. "Good job I told you an earlier time than necessary. Beth will be here soon. Happy birthday, darling."

"Oh it's lovely to see you. I know I was born at noon so there's an hour to go."

"We're still having a welcome glass of champagne when Beth arrives. I hope you've got something decent to wear. I don't want to see you in old jeans. And when does your man arrive?"

"I need a word about him. Please don't call him 'my man' or 'boyfriend' or anything like that. He's just a colleague. He's been kind to me looking after Major. Oh yes, Major's going to be a father. Alex's mare,

Moonlight, is pregnant. They are so sweet together. When I brought Major back to my place, they both pined and went off their food. I think it must be true love."

"Oh, how lovely. Will the foal belong to you or Alex?"

"Officially to Alex. I suppose I might be entitled to something if he sells it. Not that I would accept anything really."

"I see. So what are you wearing tonight?" her mother asked.

"I've got a new dress. Designer and I think it's absolutely gorgeous. And Alex gave a wonderful necklace to wear with it. So, come on, where's my pressie from you?" she laughed.

"We thought your meal and party would do instead of a present," her father teased.

"Oh well yes, of course. Sorry."

"Take no notice of him. Of course you've got a present as well. But you still have to wait till Beth gets here. Do you want to take your things upstairs?"

She hung her clothes in her old wardrobe and looked round the bedroom where she had lived all her teenage years. It had been re-decorated from the dark purple days when she had gone through that slightly strange phase in her life. It was a bland magnolia now, following the advocacy of all the home improvement gurus on television to keep things neutral.

It was still a pretty room though and her mother had kept it ready for her ever since she had first left home. Dear Mum, she thought fondly. She never stops being a mum even when her chicks have flown. Must go with the job. She heard her sister arriving and ran down the stairs.

"Hi, sister," Beth called. "Happy birthday." They hugged each other and Sarah felt the warm glow of family wrapping itself around her. There was the pop of a cork and her father arrived with a tray of glasses and a bottle of cold champagne.

"You are making such a fuss," Sarah said happily. "It's only a thirtieth birthday, not a really significant one."

They handed her presents. A lovely art book from Beth and Mike and a new digital camera from her parents.

"So you can keep us up to date with your life," her mother suggested. "You can take pictures of the new foal and e-mail them to us."

They chatted for some time until Sarah asked what needed doing. After all, she had been summoned here early to assist with the preparations for the party.

"After lunch. We're just having a shepherd's pie now. It's warming in the oven."

"So, tell me all about your new man," Beth asked. Sarah repeated the warning she had given to her mother. "Yes, yes," Beth replied. "I'll believe that one after I've met him. Description please."

"He's quite tall. Thirty-five, dark hair and grey eyes. Loves horses. Bit of a monster to work for. Too many fundamental differences between us for us ever to become really serious. He's very ambitious. Almost the most senior of the partners, as far as I can gather."

"And he lives near you and has a stable for Major. What sort of place does he live in? His own or rented?"

"Nice old place. Needs a lot of work." She didn't want to say any more as they were all certain to spend the rest of the weekend speculating.

The afternoon passed in a flurry of activity. Filling eclairs with cream. Filling vol-au-vents. Decorating the salmon her mother had cooked. Sarah was pretty useless at most of it and was given the task of wrapping cutlery in napkins.

"You can't mess that up," Beth told her sister, rudely.

Alex arrived at five o'clock, carrying an enormous bunch of flowers. Mrs. Pennyweather was quite overwhelmed. He also brought a bottle of malt whisky for her father. He too was delighted to be welcomed into their home with great enthusiasm.

"You should stick to this one," her dad whispered. "Anyone who can choose a decent malt is tops in my book."

"Dad, don't you start. Mum and Beth have already got me halfway down the aisle. We're just colleagues. Nothing more."

He gave a knowing grin and tucked his bottle away in the sideboard.

"I wasn't sure how formal we were going to be this evening," he was saying. "What's the dress code? Sarah seemed uncertain."

"Whatever you're most comfortable with. Smartish, I suppose," beamed Mrs Penny-weather. This was everything she had hoped for in a prospective husband for her daughter. Whatever Sarah said, she just knew this was the one.

"He's Certainly One To Keep Hold Of"

It was a splendid party. Sarah received many compliments about her dress and Alex's necklace was a perfect match and her parents were delighted with everything. Her father had spent much of the evening taking pictures with her new camera so she would have a record of the event. She was too busy to work out how to use it and in any case, he was keen to try it out.

Alex seemed to charm everyone and chatted easily to the other guests. When some of the younger guests started to dance, he took Sarah into his arms and proved to her and everyone watching, that he was an accomplished dancer.

"Many years of being dragged along to hunt balls and other events my parents insisted was essential to my social upbringing," he whispered to her as they danced.

"Obviously a successful upbringing," she replied.

"Have I told you how stunning you look? That dress is perfect. I love it." She smiled up at him, acknowledging that they made quite a striking couple, even if they weren't a couple.

When the guests had left, the family sat round for the traditional post-mortem. It had been a good evening, was the consensus and they all complimented Mrs Pennyweather on a splendid supper.

Beth and Mike were going home and Sarah went out to their car with them, to say goodbye.

"You were guilty of a gross understatement," Beth announced. "He's gorgeous and if I didn't have a wonderful husband of my own, I'd certainly be interested in one Alex Weston. You should snap him up. And you never mentioned that he owns Darnley Manor. I remember seeing it advertised for sale. Not only is he a lovely man, he's rich too. What's the matter with you, girl? Grab him while you can."

"We have too many differences between us. And besides, I'm not ready to settle down. It's all right for you two. You've known each other all your lives. Not everyone can be as lucky as you. I've seen too many broken marriages through work to dare take the risk. Anyway, we'll see you tomorrow. Looking forward to seeing the boys. Thanks again for the present. Night."

"Goodnight, little sister. Thirty is pretty late to put off settling down for any longer. Hang on to this one . . . he's good for you." It seemed Alex had been a hit all round.

Sarah was first down the next morning and put a pot of coffee on to brew. Her mother was next and they sat at the kitchen table nursing the mugs of hot coffee.

"So, tell me more about Alex. You seem very close," her mother said.

"Not at all really. As I keep trying to tell everyone, we're work colleagues."

"He said you'd been helping restore his house. Is it really a proper manor house? It sounds very grand."

"It's lovely, but in a terrible state of repair. It's been neglected for years and needs such a lot doing to it. But yes, I have been helping him in return for his kindness to Major."

"Well it seems to me there's a lot more to it than you're saying. We both think he's really right for you. I hope you will see it before it's too late. He's obviously smitten. I can tell the way he looks at you."

"Please, Mum. Don't keep on. If it happens it will happen, but don't hold your breath. I'm certainly not convinced."

"Why can't you be more like your sister and settle down happily? Always questioning everything."

Sarah closed her eyes, willing her mother to stop pestering.

"I'm going for a shower before the others come down. Please don't keep on at me about Alex. I knew it was going to be a mistake to invite him here this weekend."

She went upstairs and met Alex coming out of the bathroom.

"Morning. You've beaten me to it. I was just coming for a shower," she said. "Hope you slept well."

"Very well thank you. I could do with

some coffee now though. I don't start to function till I've had at least one cup."

"Mum's in the kitchen sitting by a pot of coffee. I'm sure she'll take pity on you. There's just one thing. Please don't take any notice of anything she says about us. It seems the family have earmarked you as a number one candidate for taking me off the shelf."

"That sounds good to me," he said with a slightly wicked grin. "I'll go and find some coffee right away."

After breakfast was over, they all went for a walk. Alex was pleased to discover a part of Cornwall he didn't know and enjoyed the tramp along leafy lanes and bridle paths.

He seemed at ease with everyone and Sarah watched him in a completely different environment and had to admire the way he seemed to fit in with them all. She hardly dared to admit it, but she felt herself drawing closer to him. If she relaxed and allowed it, she might just admit to finding him extremely attractive . . . even to falling in love just a little.

It was just the close family who shared lunch at one of their favourite restaurants. Beth and Mike had their three boys with them and had clearly told them to be on their best behaviour. Ethan, the six year old, was fascinated by the stranger and asked numerous questions. There was sudden silence when he asked if Alex was going to marry Auntie Sarah.

"Of course not," she replied hastily. "Alex works with me and we thought it might be nice if he came to lunch with us today." He seemed satisfied for a few minutes and then the embarrassing questions began again. They were busily fending them off when Alex's mobile rang.

"Would you excuse me?" he said. "It's my mother and she won't stop ringing till I answer."

He went outside and came back looking grim. "I'm so sorry," he told them. "She's had a fall and is panicking. I shall have to drive up there and see what's happening. I'd better leave right away. It does actually sound serious this time so I won't delay. I'm sorry about breaking up the party. Someone will give Sarah a lift home?" They had driven to the restaurant together and the parents had come in their own car. Just as well, the way things were turning out.

"Of course. Don't worry about it. We hope your mother isn't seriously hurt. What a shame." Mrs Pennyweather was most alarmed.

"Can you collect my things, Sarah? Bring

them back with you. You can drop them off at my place when you come to see Major. I'll be in touch. And thank you all so much for making me welcome and for the lovely party and lunch. Even if I didn't get beyond the starter. Bye."

He drove away at speed and Sarah waved after him feeling suddenly rather deflated.

"Have you met his mother?" Beth asked.

"Briefly. She's not the nicest or most welcoming person I've met. In fact, she's a frightful snob."

"Old or young?"

"I don't know really. Probably seventy-ish. She's tried to rule Alex since her husband died and he gets very fed up with her demands. Let's hope it isn't anything more than attention seeking this time."

"She sounds dreadful. And Alex is so nice," Beth said.

"Isn't Alex going to have his lunch?" Ethan asked. "Can I have his?"

"No and no," Mike said firmly. "You can eat your own lunch and be quiet. Your brothers are both being very good and quiet."

"I expect you'll want to get off home after we get back," Mrs Pennyweather asked her daughter. "You'll have to go and see to both horses. I doubt Alex will be back in time to feed them."

"He has a woman who comes to see to them when he's away. A sort of housekeeper who loves animals. She'll see to the dogs as well."

"She sounds like a treasure."

"Oh, yes. Everyone should have a Mrs Harper." Sarah sounded a little caustic and Beth stared at her. She raised her eyebrows but after a warning glance from Sarah, said no more.

The rest of the meal was rather more subdued, though still enjoyable. The food was beautifully cooked and it was a pleasure for them all to sit back and relax.

"Thank you all so much for making this such a special birthday. Mum, Dad, thank you. I'm so lucky to have parents like you and even the sister you gave me is pretty good."

They all hugged each other as they were leaving the restaurant and went off in their different directions.

Back at home, Sarah packed her things and went into Alex's room to collect his things. She couldn't help but sniff his toilet things as she packed them. It was like having him there with her. Subtle and very pleasing aftershave. So unlike that worn by her colleague, Charles, who was overstated in everything he did.

She planned to stop off at her own cottage and change into her old clothes, before driving over to Darnley to see the horses and leave Alex's belongings.

"Come again soon, darling," her parents insisted. "And bring Alex with you. He's certainly one to keep hold of," her mother added.

"Mum, please. Forget about matchmaking. Don't spoil it for me by pushing us into something we neither of us want. He is nice, I agree, but I'm not ready to settle down yet. Thanks again for everything. I'd better get off now."

It was a beautiful afternoon and the Sunday drivers were out in force. As she drove down the main road, she caught occasional glimpses of the sea, sparkling in the distance.

The wind farms that seemed to be growing everywhere moved their fins gracefully, lazily along the roadside. Some people hated them but Sarah loved them. They were a symbol of a greener future.

She drove back into the village and turned into the lane that led to her cottage and on towards Darnley. It was quiet and peaceful after the busy main road. It was home.

Pausing only to hang her precious dress

and change, she was soon driving towards Alex's lovely home. She went into the stables to see the horses and check they had full hay nets. They greeted her with pleasure and she fed them apples. They were clearly settled for the night.

She collected the key that was hidden in a secret place and was met by two frantic black dogs.

"Phoebe, Sophie. Hello girls." They went into a frenzy of yapping and wagging tails and leapt all over her. "You're getting too big for that now, you two." She pushed them down and bent to pet them. "Do you want to go for a run? I bet you do. Just let me unload your boss's luggage and we'll go over to the paddock."

Sarah left Alex's bag in the kitchen. She didn't want him to think she had been nosing around his home. She collected a couple of dog balls for them to chase and took them over to the paddock. They tore around as if they had been imprisoned for days, arguing over which ball to catch and play-fighting as they wrestled each other to the ground.

Sarah laughed as she watched them, being transported once more to her own childhood dogs. She'd have loved a dog of her own but knew there was no way she had room in her tiny cottage for a dog. Besides, she was out far too much and unlike Alex, did not have proper facilities for them or anyone to come and let them out. Still, she could come and share these two, pretty much whenever she liked.

There was no sign of Alex's return when she left. She put the dogs back into their room and checked the water. It was a full bowl of fresh water and signs that they had been fed left in their dog bowls.

"Bye dogs," she called out. "Be good and see you soon." She gave each of them a large biscuit from the packet on the side and left them gnawing happily away.

She was very pleased with them both and glad she had suggested getting two dogs, especially black Labradors, her favourite breed. It was dark by the time she stopped in her own drive. She wondered what was happening to Alex. It was almost ten thirty before her phone rang.

"Sarah? I've got real problems here. Mother's actually broken her leg. I'm going to have to stay here overnight. She insisted on having a cup of tea and some sandwiches while we were waiting at the hospital. Consequently, we had to wait for ages before she could have anaesthetic to have it set and plastered."

"Oh Alex, I'm so sorry. What will you do?"

"I'll have to bring her back to Darnley. They're keeping her in overnight. I'll go back to her place and pack up some stuff for her. I'll collect her from the hospital in the morning and drive straight back. I'll phone work first thing. Do you think you could you possibly go and let the animals out before you go to work?"

"Of course I will. I'll put the horses into the paddock and let the dogs out. I took Phoebe and Sophie for a run this evening. Mrs H had fed them, but I thought they'd like a bit of exercise. I'll do the same in the morning."

"Thanks very much. I hate asking you, but it is a bit of an emergency. I'll phone Mrs H and explain and get her to make up a bed for Mother. She'll be in at about nine-thirty. There's nothing much going on work-wise at the house. The builders have gone off to another job for a couple of days. I said there was nothing urgent at present. Honestly, not only does my mother spoil what was left of the weekend but she causes chaos in everyone's lives."

"I don't suppose she fell on purpose."

"I wouldn't put it past her, frankly. It was just more dramatic than she was expecting."

"Really Alex, you have a very nasty side to

your nature."

"Sorry. I just know my mother and her manipulations. I've known her all my life, don't forget. I'd better let you get to bed. You have an extra early start tomorrow. Thank you again for the weekend. I really enjoyed myself. You're so lucky to have a lovely family like yours."

"I know I'm lucky."

Despite feeling exhausted, sleep was slow to come. Trying to think what she had to do the next day made her brain race around in circles. She went down at two o'clock and made some herbal tea. She looked for her diary in her briefcase but must have left it behind on Friday.

It seemed ages ago since the party at work. In less than four hours' time, she would have to be up again and driving over to see to the horses and dogs. Though she adored them, it was sometimes such a lot of work to do. But she wouldn't swap it for anything.

When she arrived at the office, Sarah discovered she was the subject of much speculation.

"So, how did the lovely Alex get on with your family?" Poppy demanded.

"Fine. It was all fine and we had a nice weekend, thank you." She was puzzled. She didn't think she had told anyone about Alex attending her party.

"Any developments we should know about?" Poppy continued.

"I've no idea what you're talking about. We had a party at my parents' home and yes, Alex came along."

"So what's the story with his mother having an accident? How did you get home?"

"You obviously know she had an accident. He went to sort her out and is bringing her back later. I expect he told you all that. And I drove myself home. We went separately. Now, if that's everything, perhaps we might all get some work done. By the way, did Alex tell you he was at my party?"

"No. We were just fishing. Now you've confirmed what we all were guessing at."

"You two are the world's greatest gossips, Poppy and Chloe. Don't you dare start spreading any rumours. Alex and I are friends and colleagues. We happen to share a love of horses but that's it. Nothing more."

"Yes, Sarah. Of course we believe you. Don't we, Chloe?" She was spared from answering as the phone rang. The day was well and truly beginning.

Her diary was free from appointments so she was able to work on the heap of files on her desk. She was doing rather well when her phone rang. It was Chloe.

"Sarah, Mr Knowles is in reception. He sounds very upset. Is there any chance you can speak to him?"

"Of course. Send him through."

"Sarah? Miss Pennyweather. Thank you so much for seeing me without an appointment."

"Mr Knowles. Is something wrong?"

"It's my wife. I had an appointment to see my daughter on Saturday. I had someone booked to accompany us, as agreed. A mutual friend. When I got to the house, my wife said Martha had gone out for tea with a friend. Isn't there something I can do about it?"

"There certainly is plenty. Don't worry, I'm sure we can sort this out. Did she give any reasons for your daughter being away?"

"She said Martha told her she didn't want to see me. Then had the cheek to ask for a cheque to buy her some new shoes. She really should be able to manage on the settlement she has. Honestly, she's got the house and I'm paying the mortgage. She has a huge allowance each month for Martha."

"That was in lieu of a spouse maintenance, I see. So what income does she have herself?"

"She was supposed to get a job, but I don't think she's even tried anything. I suppose she must be using some of the money I send for Martha. I suspect she's got a new man actually living in the house. It isn't right, is it? That I should pay for all that?"

"Did you go through mediation at the time?"

"Well yes, and she agreed to the defined contract, I think it's called. But she isn't sticking to it."

"Maybe she doesn't realise that we could get a court order. I assume there isn't a court order in place?"

"Well no. She agreed to everything as set out in the contract framework. We didn't think we needed to go to the extra expense and well, the potential nastiness of a court order."

"If we did have to go down that route, it could even challenge the residency agreement. She could possibly end up having to forfeit the marital home agreement too. Every child has a right to see his or her father."

"You mean Martha might even live with me? I'm not sure that would work."

"Right, well I shall write to your ex-wife and set out these points. I'm sure the threat will be enough to make her change her mind about allowing you access."

"Oh Sarah, I don't know how to thank you. I hope she comes to her senses."

"And don't worry about the legal support for your case. I know it's all going through and very soon."

There were tears in the man's eyes as he left. Sarah felt quite emotional herself. Poor man.

It was afternoon before Alex arrived at the office. He was as immaculate and efficient as ever and only the dark lines under his eyes gave any indication of the stress he was suffering. It was almost the end of the day before he had time to look in at her office.

"Sorry I've not been to see you sooner. I've been playing catch-up all afternoon."

"That's no problem. What's happening? How's your mother?"

"I've installed her in the living room. She couldn't manage the stairs of course. Fortunately, Mrs Harper was able to help me down with a bed and we got her set up. She doesn't like it of course but I've put the television in there and she's got a phone beside her. Mind you, I might have to remove that. I've had six calls from her already. I fear this is going to be a difficult few weeks. Anyway, I still have things to do.

Thanks again for seeing to the dogs."

"Would you like me to go round after work? I needn't disturb your mother and I could walk the dogs and make sure the horses are all right."

"I'll manage. I'll have to get back soon. I think it's warm enough to leave the horses out at night now. Don't you agree?"

"I guess. Shame there isn't a field shelter in the paddock, then they could go inside if it rains or gets cold."

"Brilliant idea. I'll look into it. There's bound to be a local place that could provide one. I'll look on the Internet as soon as I've finished here." He left her.

How easy, when you have unlimited money, she thought. She'd had to save for ages before she could afford even a modest stable for Major. Still, it would cut down on work if the horses could stay out.

It was April and in Cornwall's relatively mild climate they should be fine. After all, many horses stayed out all the time, but neither Moonlight nor Major were used to it. It was only when sudden storms blew up that it could be a problem at this time of year.

As Sarah drove back home, she thought how much things were about to change. No longer could she go and see Major without making prior arrangements. While Mrs Weston was staying there, Alex would be busy taking care of her.

Though Mrs Harper would undoubtedly be preparing meals, his mother would be demanding his attention and company. Nor would she like the fact that he worked long hours. Rather him than me, she thought. Meanwhile, she needed to get used to a change in her own routine.

By the end of the week, Alex was looking positively haggard, especially round the eyes. Though he still presented his immaculate, well groomed appearance, the strain of looking after a demanding lady was taking its toll. On Friday evening, he rang Sarah.

"Please come for a ride with me tomorrow. I need someone to save my sanity."

"I'd be delighted, but won't your mother expect you to stay in with her?"

"I need to get some air. She'll just have to understand. I've also got the builders coming back on Monday so I'll have to get some things organised for them. More things to do inside. Can't believe all this has happened just at this point in time. Anyway, better go now. See you about ten tomorrow?"

"That's fine. Look forward to it. I've been missing my beautiful boy."

"Thank you. I didn't realise you cared."

"Major, you fool. Bye." She hung up the phone. She couldn't believe she had just called one of the senior partners a fool. She hoped Alex would take it the way it was meant.

It was a beautiful morning the next day, perfect for riding and enjoying Cornwall's countryside. It was especially beautiful in spring.

The thrift, called sea pinks by some people, were just coming into bloom and banks, stone walls and cliff tops were becoming a pink haze with the prolific little cushions of flowers. Primroses still lined hedgerows and there were many fields of daffodils shining with vast spreads of yellow.

"This is why I love Cornwall so much," Sarah said aloud as they rode along. "There's always something good to look at. When the yellows fade, blue and pink replaces them and then masses of little white wild Cornish leeks appear."

"You're quite a country girl at heart, aren't you? Despite working in the city. Well if you can call Truro a city."

"Of course it's a city," she said defensively. "It's got a cathedral."

"I do agree with you, though. Cornwall is a fabulous county. I'm so glad I managed to move down here. I challenge you to a race across the beach."

"Should you be pushing Moonlight like that?"

"Maybe not. She's very fit and healthy though. The vet examined her last week and he's very pleased with her. Reckons I can continue to ride her for a good few more weeks yet. I decided against getting another horse. The way my life is running at the moment, I really don't think I can take on anything else."

"Did the vet say when the foal is due?"

"Possibly early November."

"Exciting."

"Do you want to come back and have some lunch? Help me entertain my mother?"

"I'm not sure it's a good idea. She really doesn't like me and I don't want to upset things any more."

"You disappoint me. But, I don't blame you. She isn't a very friendly person at the best of times and there's nothing best about times at the moment."

Sarah felt guilty but she really didn't want to waste her day off being criticised by Alex's mother.

"I do have to do some shopping later. The fridge and freezer are practically empty. Do you need anything by the way? I don't mind picking up anything you're short of."

"I did an order yesterday. Mrs Harper left a list so I ordered it on-line. It seems to work all right."

"You're quite domesticated in your own way."

They rode back into the stable yard and dismounted. They collected grooming materials and gave the two horses a rub down. The two dogs were barking behind their gate. "Would you like me to take them for a run?" Sarah offered.

"It would be most helpful. I did plan to take them this afternoon but if I don't manage it, at least I'll know they've had some exercise. My mother finds them too boisterous, needless to say. Ah well, back to the grindstone. I think we have Scrabble planned for later in the day. How's that for excitement?"

"Don't know how you'll cope. I'll put the dogs back in the yard when I return. Would hate to spoil your game."

Sarah Clashes With Mrs Weston

A couple of times during the following week, Sarah drove to the Manor after work and took Major out for a short ride. She was concerned that he was missing out on exercise lately and besides, she wanted to spend time with her beloved horse.

Occasionally, she saw Alex arriving home rather late and gave him a wave. She didn't speak to him and felt that anything that might have developed in the way of a relationship was slipping away. She scarcely saw him at work and even realised that the gossip was dying down. She was going out very little and felt somewhat isolated.

When Poppy suggested an evening at the cinema to see one of the current blockbuster movies, she leapt at the chance. Several of the staff went along and they all went for pizzas afterwards.

"That was a good evening," she commented as they all said their goodbyes. "Let's do it again sometime." They agreed and Poppy walked back to her car with her.

"You seem a bit down lately. Is anything wrong?"

"Not really. Just a dull patch in my life."

"The gorgeous Alex neglecting you?"

"He's still got his sick mother staying with him. My horse is still stabled over there and as his mother doesn't approve of me, I'm just not getting out as much as I was."

"Why don't you take your horse back to your place?"

"Cos he's in love with Alex's horse and they both fret when they're apart."

"I didn't know horses could be like that."

"These two can. Both went off their food and behaved like typical teenagers with massive crushes."

"Good heavens," Poppy said. "Sounds worse than having kids around. Better go now. It's past my bedtime."

"Night," Sarah replied. "See you tomorrow. And thanks for including me tonight."

Her answering machine was flashing when she got home.

"Please call me. I've got problems." Alex sounded desperate.

She dialled his mobile, assuming that wouldn't disturb Mrs Weston if she was asleep. She remembered him saying she had a phone nearby and didn't want to wake her. Alex picked up immediately.

"Hi, it's Sarah. Is something wrong?"

"Certainly is. Maddy, Mrs Harper, has handed in her notice. Immediate effect."

"Oh no. Can she do that? Catastrophe."

"And the workmen walked off the site today."

"Don't tell me. Your mother?"

"Got it in one. She's been complaining all week. Cups of tea every few minutes and then it's not strong enough. Coffee and that's too strong. And the meat was tough. The vegetables were overcooked. She hadn't cleaned the room properly. Mrs H has had as much as she can take.

"Mother hates the workmen banging about, as she puts it. Complains the dogs are barking and when they got into her room, she said they'd leapt on her and put her health back by several weeks. I'm at my wits' end. I can't manage without Mrs H to run things."

"Can't you persuade her to stay on for a while? Just till you find someone else or even till you can get your mother back home?"

"The latter is probably going to take weeks. I doubt there's anyone else around here with Mrs H's flexibility."

"What about some sort of nursing home? Just till she's on her feet again."

"I suggested that when I first brought her here. I told her she'd be left an awful lot while I was at work but she wanted to be here. A nursing home was the last thing she would accept. Can't say I blame her, really."

"So, how can I help?"

"I wondered if you could possibly have the dogs to stay with you for a bit. That would be one thing less."

"Oh Alex, I'd love to but my place is just too small. And they are used to being in and out all day. I don't even have a proper fence round my garden. Poor Phoebe and Sophie. I could come over after work, whenever I leave early enough, that is and I could take them out. I could do the horses' feeds as well."

"Thanks very much. That would be a start anyway. I don't want to burden you too much. If she has less to do, Mrs H might stay for a while at least. I'll try to make sure you can get away promptly each evening. Extra secretarial help might make a difference and someone to take on more of your filing."

"And my targets? Any help offered there?"

"Let's not go there. You know my thoughts on that."

"And you know mine. I'll see to the animals tomorrow and we'll catch up at some point."

"Thanks very much. Sorry to burden you with my problems."

"OK. I'll do what I can, but that won't

solve all your problems."

"I'll be late in tomorrow. I'll have to try and smooth things over with Maddy. I persuaded her to stay till the end of the week. Oh heavens. I've just been so reliant on her. Dratted woman."

"Who? Your mother or Mrs H?"

"Both I suppose. Currently it's Maddy who's making me mad. Sorry. You must need to get to bed. I'll see you tomorrow sometime."

It was the start of a few hectic weeks. Mrs Harper left and Alex managed to get someone else to come in a few hours a week to clean and he did all the cooking. He was taking work home to make up for leaving early.

As to Mrs Weston's progress, there seemed to be little happening. She was getting around a little bit on her crutches but from what Alex said, it seemed to be taking a very long time for her to recover at all.

Sarah's client, Mr Knowles, seemed to have re-established contact with his daughter. The threat of a court order had brought his wife to her senses and visits had resumed in an acceptable way.

"You'll never believe what my ex-wife had told Martha," he said on the phone, one day. "She'd only told her it was me who didn't want to see her. Poor little kid had cried herself to sleep night after night."

"I can believe it. So many couples with marital breakdown use their kids as blackmail tools. Very distressing all round."

"I've told Martha that any time she feels sad, she must phone me and I'll come and see her. Oh and there is another man living with her. Makes me furious to think I'm renting a horrible flat and someone else has got my home."

Sarah felt desperately sorry for the man, but the financial settlement had included the house and unless they applied for a reassignment of the property, which he might not win because of Martha living there, he had to accept the situation.

"I could pursue this is if you want me to."

"I'll leave it for now. I've applied for another job and now you've got my maintenance payments sorted, things are definitely easier. You've been brilliant, Sarah. I only wish I'd been in touch with you from the start of all this. Thanks again."

At least things had improved and he was much happier and it was nice to get his compliment.

It was now summer and the county was filling up with tourists for the holiday season. It meant that the dogs couldn't be let off on the beaches, in fact there were a number of beaches where dogs were banned altogether during the summer months.

"I gather the extra dog walking is getting to you, just a bit?" Poppy asked one day when she saw Sarah looking a bit washed-out.

"It's everything really. I seem to do nothing but work, exercise the dogs and horses and go home and fall into bed."

"And what is Alex doing while all this is going on?"

"Trying to persuade his mother it's time she went home, basically. He had a wonderful housekeeper person who gave in her notice when the grande dame decided she wasn't any good. I don't think either of us can go on at this pace for much longer."

"And how are things between the two of you? I must say, I was having high hopes for the pair of you at one time."

"Some chance. With his full-time chaperone breathing down his neck, I daren't have so much as cup of coffee in his kitchen. The work on the house is all at a standstill. Nothing has been done for weeks now. I think all his workmen have gone on to another job permanently. At least he's eased off on my failure to reach targets over the past few weeks. And the horses are out all the time now, so that's a bit less work. Sorry. I shouldn't be moaning. Not a word to anyone else, please."

"Course not. I may be a gossip at times but I consider this is totally confidential and wouldn't breathe a word to anyone. Maybe we should organise a meal out and cheer you up a bit?"

"Haven't got the time for a while yet. But thanks anyway. If I manage an evening off, I'll let you know."

"I must say, Alex himself does seem a bit grumpy lately, but if he's a carer as well as a lawyer you can't really blame him."

Sarah was returning the dogs to the house one evening, when Alex arrived home a bit earlier than usual.

"Come and have a drink," he invited. "You certainly deserve it."

"Oh, no thanks. I don't want to intrude on you and your mother."

"Please come in. I don't seem to have seen you in ages. Except passing in the corridors at work, which hardly counts. I've got a very good bottle of Burgundy I need to share with someone and you're the someone."

"Well, just one glass maybe. I'm driving so it has to be just one."

They went into the kitchen. The room had somehow lost some of the sparkle. It was nothing tangible but it didn't look quite as inviting as it did at first.

"What are you looking at?" Alex asked.

"I was wondering what's changed, but I can't quite tell."

"It's a bit grubby. Maddy's replacement doesn't believe in elbow grease or much in the way of cleaning materials, come to that."

"So how much longer is your mother going to be staying?"

"Not much longer. I'm sure she's well able to return home but she prefers being here, is the long and short of it. Now," he said as he poured the wine, "See what you think of that."

She sniffed it as her father had taught her to do and breathed in the heady aroma. She swirled it gently in the over-sized glass and took a first sip.

"Mmm, that is good," she announced positively. "Very good indeed. Expensive no doubt."

"A bit," he conceded, "but well worth it. I've laid some down in the cellar. A good offer from my wine merchant."

Sarah perched on a stool and held the glass between her hands, savouring the wine. The door opened and Mrs Weston came in. Sarah leapt to her feet and stood awkwardly near to Alex.

"Oh, I see you have company. Don't mind me. I just came to get myself a glass of water."

With great drama, she crossed to the fridge on her crutches and made a great show of balancing as she drew out some water from the chiller. Wobbling violently, she almost fell against the table and just managed to put the glass down without dropping it on the floor.

"Can I help?" offered Sarah.

"Don't trouble yourself. I will manage somehow."

"Do you want a glass of wine, Mother?" Alex asked wearily, pouring one as he spoke.

"Well it would be nice, if it isn't too much trouble. I won't intrude though as you are entertaining a guest." She managed to sound just a little feeble and pathetic but there was a glint in her eyes that made Sarah feel certain it was all an act.

"Sit down, Mother and don't try to act the martyr."

Sarah was surprised at his tone. "Here you are. Sarah was just returning the dogs after walking them for me. I was sharing some wine in gratitude for all she does."

"I expect you pay her well enough," the

older woman snapped.

"She does it out of kindness, Mother. After you single-handedly caused Mrs Harper to leave, someone had to help me. I'm frantically busy at work and you take a lot of looking after."

"You'll be old and frail one day and I hope then, you'll regret being so unkind to me."

"Please, don't start that again. You've been here for weeks now and it's time you were getting back to your own home."

Mrs Weston swung round to glare at Sarah.

"You've put him up to this. Can't wait to get your hands on his money and move in here. That's it, isn't it?"

Sarah went white. She put the half-empty glass down on the table and turned to leave.

"Goodnight, Alex. I'll see you at the office sometime."

Feeling ready to burst into tears, she rushed across the yard and got into her car. She drove away rapidly, seeing Alex through her rear view mirror, as he was rushing after her. She saw him hold up his hands in a gesture of defeat.

"Horrible woman," she muttered. "How dare she accuse me of all those things? I've put myself out for weeks to make sure the animals were all cared for. Never asked for anything in return and she dares to say that. She can just stew."

She arrived home and sat down and did in fact shed a few tears. She never even got to finish that wonderful glass of wine. She would have loved to be a fly on the wall and hear what was going on back at Darnley Manor House that evening.

If she had been, she would certainly not have enjoyed Mrs Weston's vicious comments about her. Alex was furious with his mother and the two of them had the row to end all rows. He was exhausted by her demands and the length of time she had been staying with him . . . imposing on him.

Finally, he had snapped and was insisting on taking his mother to see the specialist, tomorrow if he could arrange it. If the consultant said she was fit to go home, then that was what he planned. He agreed to get an agency to provide a carer for her and said it was up to her to make it work.

If she persisted in causing her carers to leave, the way she had made Maddy Harper leave, then it was up to her to manage for herself. She was not at all happy. She had enjoyed being waited on and even liked playing the Lady of the Manor, a role she believed she was made for. She had even been planning to create an apartment for her own use.

One day when she was in the house alone for a long period, she had easily managed to get herself up the stairs and select a couple of rooms she would suggest could be converted for her use. She had said nothing to her son about her secret plans, intending to make her suggestion when she admitted to being better.

After this row, she knew she had probably burned her boats. He was not showing any sympathy to her, even when she had feebly asked for help to return to her room.

When Sarah arrived at the office next morning, she asked Alex's secretary, Julia, if she could have an appointment to see him during the morning. She knew private business should not intrude into working hours but she needed to know what had happened the previous evening.

"He's not in this morning and I'm not sure if he'll be available later in the day. I'll let you know."

"Do you know why?" Sarah asked anxiously.

"I believe it's a family problem," Julia replied cautiously.

"OK. Thanks. I'll catch him later maybe." It was difficult to concentrate but her stream of appointments kept her busy and allowed her to stop worrying a little.

Alex did not come to work all day and she was hesitant about going to his home that evening to feed and exercise the animals. She finally plucked up courage to call his mobile. It went straight to voice mail. She called the home number, keeping her fingers crossed that Mrs Weston didn't answer. It didn't work.

"Darnley Manor. Mrs Weston speaking."

"Ah, Mrs Weston. It's Sarah. I was wondering if Alex is available?"

"No he isn't. And he doesn't want to speak to you. I was told not to take your calls and if I had known it was you, I would certainly not have answered."

"Very well. I was merely inquiring if I was needed to walk his dogs this evening."

"He is walking them himself. Goodbye." She hung up and Sarah was left staring angrily at her own phone.

"Great," she said angrily to nobody. She hoped Alex really was walking the dogs. They shouldn't have to suffer because their humans had problems. She wondered whether to go and take Major out for a ride but didn't want to run the risk of having an encounter with Mrs Weston.

Instead, she settled for cooking herself

some supper and settling down to watch television. She was about to have an early night when her phone rang. At last, it was Alex's number showing on her phone.

"Hi Sarah. Is everything all right?"

"I suppose so."

"I missed you walking the dogs this evening."

"Really? Your mother said you were doing it and I wasn't needed. I called earlier to ask if I should come over. She said I wasn't required and that you had told her not to speak to me. I just didn't want to cause you anymore difficulties."

"Honestly, I shall be guilty of doing something drastic if I don't take action very soon. Naturally, I said nothing of the sort to her. I did walk the dogs but as I wasn't in the office today, I had time. They are fine but I'm sorry you were upset by my wretched mother.

"Well, it's all in hand now. I took her to the consultant this morning and he says there is absolutely no reason why she can't walk properly. He's taken the crutches away and organised some intensive physiotherapy for her. I've organised a taxi to deliver her to the department each morning for the rest of the week and I'm taking her back to her home on Saturday."

"Goodness. What a busy day you've had. Will she manage?"

"I've got a care agency going in twice a day to help her. If she sacks anyone who tried to help, then it's up to her to manage alone. I've had enough. She's been hanging on for much too long and it wasn't even necessary. She's pretty lonely where she lives, but that's her own fault. She manages to alienate most people."

"I see," Sarah murmured.

"And ignore what she said. I wouldn't dream of not speaking to you, ever. In fact, I was hoping we might return to some sort of friendship once this mess is all sorted out. You've been fantastic all these weeks, taking my dogs out and seeing to the horses."

"No problem, but it might be nice to return to normal life again. I've just felt so exhausted and as if there's nothing more in life than work."

"Well, I have one more favour to ask you. Would you look after the animals on Saturday? I need to take Mother home and settle her in. I plan to stay overnight and do the shopping etcetera. The agency are sending someone round on Sunday for me to show them the routine and also explain about the exercise regime and all that entails. She

216

should be able to drive again in a few weeks so that will mean she can get out again."

"Of course I'll help out at the weekend. I might even manage a ride for once, without feeling terrorised if I catch a glimpse of your mother."

Sarah thoroughly enjoyed herself at the weekend. She took a picnic lunch and spent the entire day at the Manor with the horses and the dogs. Moonlight was certainly showing her pregnancy now and seemed in perfect health.

She took her for a short ride round the paddock and along the lane. The mare seemed to enjoy the change and behaved beautifully despite her different rider. She took her back to the paddock after further grooming and then went for a longer ride on Major. The beach was quiet so she was able to go for a good gallop. Her own beautiful horse responded and tossed his mane in delight at the freedom.

After the horses had been fed, it was the turn of the dogs for a long walk. She took them into one of Alex's fields and did some training exercises with them. They were responsive and seemed to enjoy the extra attention.

"You're as much my dogs as Alex's, aren't you?" she said to them as she petted them.

"Never mind, your boss will soon be back into his old routine and you'll get all the fuss you need." They both barked in delight, almost as if they knew exactly what was being said. She took them back and fed them, leaving them the run of the kitchen and the utility room.

"I'll be back before bed time to let you girls out again. Be good now." She petted them both and gave them an extra biscuit and locked the doors. The house was quiet and empty. She resisted the temptation to look around, knowing she would prefer Alex to show her himself. There could have been little progress since she had last seen everywhere and Mrs Weston had been using the lounge as her bedroom for some time.

She hoped that this was the end of a very difficult few weeks.

A Chance For Happiness

Alex arrived back during the afternoon on Sunday. He looked completely exhausted as he walked up Sarah's drive.

"Hi. I saw your car there so thought I'd stop to say thank you and check all is well at the Manor."

"Come in. You look as if you could do with a cup of something."

"Tea would be great. Thanks."

"I was just going back to check on everyone. Walk the girls and so on. I went this morning and made sure they were OK. I'll put the kettle on."

He slumped down on the armchair and Sarah brought a mug of tea for him. "You look shattered."

"I am. I got Mother settled and filled the freezer. Changed the bed and did a load of washing. The carer looks as if she'll be all right. No-nonsense type but I bet she won't last long. Mother is bound to find something wrong. But I've told her I'm washing my hands of it all now. I'll pay the bill but I'm not going back even if she claims to be dying. I just feel so used. The consultant said she could have been walking properly weeks ago."

"She obviously enjoyed living at your place."

"Put the name Manor in front of anywhere and she'll think it's her due. I'd better be going. You don't need another trip out with my dogs."

"We could go together. It might do you good to get some fresh air."

"All right. Then maybe we go and get something to eat?"

"I'd offer to cook, but I doubt a frozen

fish pie would be very enticing."

"Is that what you live on?"

"I do cook fresh vegetables with it."

"You certainly need taking in hand, my girl. I'd take you for a slap-up meal if I wasn't so exhausted. For now, it will have to be the village pub. What do you say?"

"Sounds good to me. Then we can catch up on all the gossip."

"And maybe make a few plans for the coming weeks? Months? Years?"

Sarah stared at him. What was he suggesting?

"Let's plan to go for a walk and have something to eat at the pub. That will do for now."

They walked for an hour, chatting amicably. The tiredness lines fell away from Alex's face as he gradually relaxed. They stopped by the paddock to pet the horses. Major stood protectively close to his lovely companion and they nuzzled each other contentedly.

"It's almost as if they both know exactly what is happening."

"Now, shall we get these two home and go and eat? I'm starving. I'd better get my stuff out of the car first and maybe I should change. Do you mind waiting?"

"I should have brought my car. I'll need

to stop off and change as well. I'm a bit grubby."

"No problem. I won't be long."

They stopped at her cottage and Alex lay back on her little sofa. When she came down again, he was fast asleep, his long legs hanging over the arms. She stared down at him, almost unwilling to wake him.

She could imagine him looking a bit like that as a child, relaxed and without the strength that usually showed in his face. If she left him for long, he would be very stiff on her small sofa.

"Alex," she whispered, gently shaking him. "Wake up, Alex." His eyelids fluttered and slowly opened. He jerked up when he realised where he was and sat up, rubbing his neck.

"You need a bigger sofa," he complained.

"Sorry. I didn't buy it for someone of your size to sleep on. This is a tiny room. So, are we going to eat or is it to be frozen fish pie?"

"No offence to your fish pie, but I think the pub beckons. I mustn't be late though. My mother certainly takes it out of me."

It was a pleasant evening. Both of them were tired so once they had eaten, Alex dropped her off at home and they parted. He took her hand as she was getting out of the car and leaned over to kiss her.

"I'm so grateful to have you in my life. I just hope my mother hasn't done too much to put you off me . . . well my family."

"As long as you don't really believe I'm after your money, I guess I can cope."

"Of course I don't. My mother thinks anyone and everyone is only after the money. Not exactly flattering. I have no illusions about myself. I can be very difficult."

"Oh, I know," Sarah said vehemently. "But only at work. I can really dislike you at work sometimes, but maybe you'll soften in time."

"On that note, I'll say goodnight. And I promise, I will try to be more understanding. It's a difficult role I'm trying to fill. However popular Ken was . . . is, I have seen the whole picture. He isn't a good manager and the firm is not viable at present. I've got quite a task ahead to pull it round without shedding too many people."

"Wow. I didn't realise there was that sort of problem. All the same, no . . . I'm not getting started on that. You need a good night's sleep."

"You're not kidding. My mother's sofa is marginally better than yours but not much. We'll have a proper dinner soon and a real discussion. So much I want to say to you, dear Sarah. Good night."

She went inside and touched her cheek where he had kissed her. For so long, she had pushed away all thoughts of settling down and all thoughts that she and Alex might even share a future.

He had certainly made an impression on her family. Whenever either her parents or sister had spoken to her since her birthday, they had asked after him, but she fobbed them off. Or so she thought. The next week might be interesting.

It was the following Saturday before they really had the chance to talk. Sarah went to the manor to see Alex and the horses.

"Remember the dinner we never had all those months ago? I booked us a table there for this evening. I do hope you're free?" Alex said.

"That would be lovely. Thank you. I never have tried that place. I think you took your mother in my place, didn't you?"

"I did. She found fault with most of it, but I loved it and think you will too. It's less difficult to get a table now it's been open for awhile, so I booked it."

The food was indeed perfect and the setting quite magical. It was getting cooler in the evenings now, so they were able to watch the moody sea through the wide windows, rather than sit outside.

"I could watch the sea forever, I think," Sarah said dreamily. "It has mesmeric qualities and always presents a different picture."

"It's quite rough tonight. The white foam looks very bright against the dark. Sarah, we need to talk. Seriously, I mean."

"OK. I'm listening."

"You must know I am very serious about you. I really believe there could be a future for us. Though I confess to being uncertain about the word love itself, I do believe we have a lot of love to share."

"You sound like Prince Charles. The 'whatever love is' remark he made on his engagement to Diana."

"It was a brave statement. Very brave of him under the circumstances. But you know, I've heard so many definitions of love. For me, I think it's this. I want to be with you all of the time it's possible. I wake up thinking of you and my heart gives a jolt whenever we meet at work. I drive past your cottage and see the lights on and think of you inside, watching television or listening to music. I want to be inside with you. Share you."

Sarah found herself blushing at his words. It may not have been the most romantic speech she had ever heard but she knew it came from his heart.

She stared down at the tablecloth and then looked into his steely grey eyes, now softened into a mistier colour altogether.

"I do feel pretty much the same. I admit, I haven't felt this way about anyone else before. Is it love? It may be but I'm not sure. I can imagine living my life with you. As you said once before, we share so much in common. I'm scared though. I'm scared that it's possible that one day we could grow to hate each other. All the people I deal with in divorce cases, once loved each other. If there are children involved, think how much pain they would have to suffer."

"Can we spend more quality time together and see where it goes? Who can tell, we might discover what real love is? I couldn't bear the thought of being anywhere other than with you."

"Sounds good to me. Let's not make any huge commitment at this stage. See where we go."

He reached for her hand and gently kissed her finger tips, his eyes intent on hers.

The next few weeks were busy at work and Sarah and Alex spent as much leisure time together as they were able. There was a definite closeness growing between them and Sarah was even beginning to believe in love itself. She said nothing to Alex, waiting for him to be the first to discuss his feelings again.

The workmen had returned to Darnley and the renovations were well underway again. Sarah was giving her advice and suggestions but was slightly less involved than she had been.

The wonderful Mrs Harper had also been persuaded to return to work and so the load was lightened all round. She took the dogs out for some exercise well before it was dark so that Alex was able to finish his work without too much stress.

Despite her doubts about his working methods, Sarah had to admit that Alex was getting results. The whole office building was looking better and included the promised interview room available to all the staff when needed.

The evenings drew in and the horses spent much of the time in the stable. Moonlight and Major were close to each other but still had their own areas in separate loose boxes. It was safer to leave them slightly apart, in case Moonlight began her labour prematurely and Major was somehow disturbed. When the time was closer, they planned to leave the pair in separate stables, not that they would like it, but it seemed sensible.

Sarah was in the depths of sleep one night towards the end of November when her phone rang. Sleepily she lifted the receiver.

"Sarah? It's Alex. Moonlight's giving birth right now. I think she's nearly there, if you want to come over."

"Thanks. On my way." She tugged on thick trousers and a fleece over the top of her pyjamas and rushed out to her car. She was almost shaking with excitement and feeling very wobbly at being woken from such a deep sleep.

There were lights on outside the buildings and she stopped outside the yard gates. Major whinnied when he heard her and she scarcely stopped to do more than stroke his nose before going into the stable. Moonlight was lying down and beside her lay a tiny foal, chestnut like her father, but with a white blaze between her eyes.

"I'm too late," Sarah said disappointed. "But isn't it gorgeous?"

"She certainly is. It was very quick. I phoned the vet and described what was happening. He said he'll come if we think we need him but he was confident all was going to plan."

"Look at the little star on her forehead. We should call her Star or Starlight."

"Ursa Major, perhaps. Take account of her father." They both smiled. "She really has to be Starlight, doesn't she?"

The little creature staggered to her feet and her mother raised herself up. She cleaned the foal some more and it reached beneath her seeking milk. Major whinnied from next door and Moonlight raised her head and whinnied back.

"He wants to be a part of it, but I think he's best left where he is for now. Hey, well done girl," she said, patting the horse's neck.

They both went out of the stable and shut the door on the new little family. "Oh Alex, isn't it wonderful?" Her eyes were filling with tears.

He caught her hand and pulled her close. He kissed her cold lips and then led her inside the house.

"Come on. A hot drink is needed. You're freezing."

She shivered and agreed.

The kitchen was cosy and warm, just as she remembered it that first time she had been inside the house all those months ago.

"You can tell Mrs H is back. It has that sparkle again. Oh, thanks," she added as he handed her a hot chocolate. "Just what I needed."

"Sarah," Alex began softly, "I think I know

what love means. Seeing you in the stable, watching Moonlight with such wonder, I suddenly knew that I want you here with me all the time. Will you marry me, Sarah?"

"I don't think I have any choice in the matter. We are both a bit overwrought and emotional tonight but we have become very good friends lately, haven't we? I think love and marriage need to be based on true friendship and now, I think I agree. What I feel for you is indeed true love. And you're my best friend as well."

"What more could I ask? When can we tell everyone?"

"I'd like to keep it to ourselves for a while. I'd like to tell my parents face to face for a start."

"There is one problem. Can you bear to marry me, when I have a mother like mine?"

"That is a bit of a deterrent but I'm marrying you, not your mother. As long as we can limit her visits and that she knows she'll be asked to leave if she continues to make nasty remarks about me."

"Agreed. Now, I think we better get some sleep. There's not much of the night left and I do have a hearing in court tomorrow morning."

Exhausted, Sarah drove back to her cottage. Quite a night. "And," she whispered as she settled back into her bed, "I do believe I've become engaged to be married."

As Christmas approached, Alex and Sarah faced the eternal problem of where were they to spend the holiday. Mrs Weston couldn't really be left alone and Sarah's parents would expect her home. They had kept their secret so far and no-one at work suspected a thing.

"I've had a brilliant idea," Alex announced. "Why don't we invite everyone here? There will be room for them, even if all the bedrooms aren't properly finished. Then we can make the big announcement over Christmas dinner. What do you think?"

"It sounds wonderful, but I can't even think of cooking for that lot. Do you mean Beth and the kids as well?"

"Why not? I'm sure Maddy Harper would come in. She claims to have no family commitments so she can come and cook and share the meal with us. Please say yes. I think it will be terrific fun. We can have a huge tree in the hall."

"My mum will have already made cakes and puddings. It's what she does."

"Great. She can bring them with her."

"OK. I'll phone them and see how they feel about it."

Naturally, everyone thought it was a brilliant idea.

"I've been longing for an invitation to see the place since you first mentioned it," her mother said. "How exciting. And Beth and her family. Are they invited too?"

"Of course. It's a vast place, even if some of it won't have been finished. Will you bring one of your puddings please?"

"I was going to offer. I've already made puddings and cakes, oh and also mincemeat. Leave all that to me. I shall be delighted to think I've made a contribution. What does Beth say to the idea?"

"I wanted to run it past you first, Mum. If you were against the idea, there would be no point."

"And is there anything you want to tell us?"

"Of course not. I don't know what you mean," Sarah said, stifling a smile.

Beth's response was very much the same. Great enthusiasm and the expected query about there being any news.

"The only problem with all of this is Mrs Weston. Naturally she has to be included and she is a bit of a monster. Alex assures me he will threaten her with being deported if she says a single nasty word. Easily said, but she may be grateful enough not to be

231

left on her own and so behave herself."

"I'm sure we'll cope. There are more of us than her, anyway. Leave Dad with her. He can charm anyone in five minutes flat."

"Maybe," Sarah said doubtfully.

The next couple of weeks were spent in frantic activity. Work at the office was slowing down so they were able to leave earlier some evenings. Alex had ordered a mountain of decorations, a huge tree and had been driving his decorators like a man possessed. New beds had been arriving and chests of drawers and wardrobes were taken into each room.

"Pillows," he announced suddenly. "I've forgotten pillows. Where can I get dozens of pillows?"

"Don't panic," Sarah calmed him. "I'll order some on-line. Let's do a tour round and make sure there isn't anything else. You might have forgotten any number of things, working on this massive scale."

By the time they had finished, she had a long list, including bath mats for the extra bathrooms, a set of sheets for one room that was also missing curtains and four bedside lamps.

"Right. I'll order it all to be delivered as soon as possible." She sat at his computer and made her choices. It was all very simple and half-an-hour later, it was all done. She sat back and looked at the man she now knew for certain that she loved. He was carrying a tray of tea and set it down on the table beside her.

"I don't know how we're going to fit everything into the time we've got. They all arrive on Christmas Eve, so between now and then we have to put up decorations, make sure the house is ready for all these guests, buy enough food and most important, I need to buy you a ring.

"I was planning to surprise you, but when I started looking in the jewellers, I realised I have no idea which stone you would actually like. You'll be wearing it for a good many years so it has to be right. Am I very unromantic if I suggest you come with me to choose it?"

"Oh Alex, I'd really like that. I was wondering if you were planning something for my Christmas present. I'd love to be with you to choose it. Thank you."

There was a look of complete relief on his face.

"Thank you. I was so afraid you would expect it to be a surprise and then hate it."

The following afternoon, after work, Alex took her to the biggest jewellers in town. He had asked them to have some trays ready for her to look at.

She stared at the dazzling array of rings resting on their black velvet cushions. It was difficult to choose, but she decided on a simple ring with three diamonds.

"It looks very expensive," she said doubtfully. "Are you sure?"

"If that's the one you would like, that is the one you shall have. Don't worry about the cost. But you can't have it till Christmas day."

"Thank you, Alex. It's so beautiful."

"If you were a kitten, you'd be purring," he said taking her hand fondly as they walked back to the car.

"We should get back. There's one large tree waiting for attention."

The office was closed the day before Christmas Eve. She had taken her belongings over to the room Alex had prepared for her to stay over the holiday.

They made an early start organising everything. Maddy Harper was coming in early to make up beds and make sure everywhere was clean. She was also invited to stay over, as she was going to be doing all the cooking. She seemed very grateful to be included and more than earned her stay by working frantically in the kitchen.

"This is going to be a fabulous, old-fashioned family Christmas," Alex kept saying, revelling in the whole business.

Mrs Weston and Sarah's family were all arriving after lunch on Christmas Eve. There was to be a simple dinner in the evening and hopefully, an early night for Beth's children. Everything was ready. Presents were wrapped and Alex had lit a huge log fire in the lounge. The downstairs rooms were all finished and they went from room to room checking everything was in place. Alex and Sarah held hands and beamed at each other.

"We did it!" she said. The dogs began to bark frantically. "Someone's arriving, I think."

It was Sarah's family arriving together.

"We decided to drive down in convoy so we'd all find it easily. What a fabulous place," Mrs Pennyweather chirped excitedly.

"Come in. Welcome." Alex looked suddenly shy. He had never known a proper family and felt a little overcome by the magnitude of being host to so many people. Everyone piled into the hall and gasped at the magnificent huge tree.

"Wow," exclaimed Ethan. "I've never seen such a big tree. It's like a forest. Must have taken hours to decorate it."

"Quite a while," Alex agreed.

At last, Mrs Weston arrived and came in looking perturbed by the large number of people filling the place.

"We're just about to have cups of tea and mince pies. My mother's made them and they're highly recommended. Come and sit by the fire, Mrs Weston," Sarah invited. "I'd like to introduce you to my parents."

Without protest or comment, she sat down and shook hands with everyone. Mr Pennyweather sat beside her and chatted as if she was an old friend. They overheard her saying to him after a short while, "Call me Emma. We can't be so formal when we're all under one roof."

Sarah's jaw dropped. Good old Dad. Beth was right, his charm was certainly working.

It was a most enjoyable evening and three excited little boys were taken to their room and hung stockings at the end of their bed. Mince pies, a glass of sherry and a carrot for the reindeer were duly left near the tree and even Mrs Weston entered the spirit of the little ceremony.

"I never ever did that," Alex whispered to his almost fiancée. "But we'll do it with our kids, won't we?"

"You have a charming family Sarah, my dear," Mrs Weston said quietly, leaving Sarah gasping in amazement. Was this a breakthrough?

They didn't manage to wait till Christmas dinner for their announcement. They were all sitting down for coffee after the children were in bed.

"So," Beth said loudly. "When are you going to tell us your news?"

"I don't know what you mean," Sarah protested.

"You two are looking as if you'll burst any minute. And you can't take your eyes off each other and you keep brushing your fingers whenever you pass each other. Come on."

Alex and Sarah looked at each other and laughed softly.

"All right everyone. Sarah has agreed to make me the happiest of men. She's going to let me keep the foal all to myself." Everyone laughed and even Mrs Weston raised a flicker of a smile. "OK. Yes, we're going to be married. Sarah, you can have your present now after all, even if it isn't Christmas yet." He took the ring box from his pocket and slipped the lovely diamonds on her finger.

Right on cue, Maddy Harper came in with a tray of glasses and a magnum of champagne.

"I gather you need this now rather than

tomorrow?"

They all raised their glasses.

"To Alex and Sarah."

"To love, whatever that is," Alex said with a grin as he put his arms round the woman he knew he truly loved.

We hope you have enjoyed this Large Print book. Other Thorndike, Wheeler, Kennebec, and Chivers Press Large Print books are available at your library or directly from the publishers.

For information about current and upcoming titles, please call or write, without obligation, to:

Publisher
Thorndike Press
10 Water St., Suite 310
Waterville, ME 04901
Tel. (800) 223-1244

or visit our Web site at:

http://gale.cengage.com/thorndike

OR

Chivers Large Print
published by AudioGO Ltd
St James House, The Square
Lower Bristol Road
Bath BA2 3SB
England
Tel. +44(0) 800 136919
email: info@audiogo.co.uk
www.audiogo.co.uk

All our Large Print titles are designed for easy reading, and all our books are made to last.